Anges' Answer

The Willoughby Witches

(Book Four)

by

Terri Reid

Agnes' Answer

The Willoughby Witches
(Book Four)

by Terri Reid

The author would like to thank all those who have contributed to the creation of this book: Richard Reid, Peggy Hannah, Mickey Claus, Terrie Snyder, and Ruth Ann Mulnix. And especially to the wonderful readers who are starting this whole new adventure with me, thank you all!

Chapter One

(45 years earlier)

As an array of golden, red, and brown leaves floated down on the narrow, country road from their perches high on the towering maple, birch, and oak trees, a school bus slowed to a stop in front of the old farmhouse. The doors slid open, and immediately the quiet countryside was filled with the sounds of mocking taunts and raucous laughter. On the heels of the noise, a five-year-old girl, Agnes Willoughby, stepped purposely down the steps and, with head held high, slowly walked forward.

"Witch, witch, fell in a ditch. Found a penny and thought she was rich!"

She recognized the voice; Billy Stoughton had set his foul sights on her the moment she'd started school, and following his lead, the other children on the bus had set out to bully her.

"I'm a Willoughby," she murmured softly. "And they can't hurt me."

She reached the half-way point between the road and the porch when the bus door slid closed, and the rumbling vehicle continued down the road. But Agnes didn't let down her guard, just in case someone was watching from the back window. Instead, she held her back ramrod straight and clenched her jaw to hold back the tears.

In front of her, the front door swung open, and her mother stepped out on the porch. The concern in her eyes was palpable, and she hurried forward to the top of the steps. "Agnes," her mother sighed, her voice filled with regret. "What happened today?"

Agnes looked up, green eyes meeting gray, and took a deep breath. "I'm fine," she lied. "It was just a hard day at kindergarten."

Sympathy, and something else Agnes didn't quite recognize, washed over her mother's face. Climbing down the stairs, her mother knelt in front of Agnes and wrapped

6

her arms around her. "I'm so sorry it was a hard day," she consoled gently. "Would you like to talk about it over grilled cheese sandwiches?"

Agnes' serious expression lightened, and she nodded slowly. "Are they cut into stars and moons?" she asked.

Her mother nodded. "Of course," she replied. "And I made tomato-basil soup so we could dip them."

Agnes took a step back and eyed her mother suspiciously. "Mom," she said with a sigh. "I can handle this. You don't have to treat me like a baby "

Shaking her head, her mother gathered her in her arms again. "I know you can," she agreed. "And, even if you had a wonderful day at kindergarten, grilled cheese is always a good idea, don't you think?"

Agnes laid her head against her mother's chest and let the warmth and love seep into her little body. She inhaled deeply, smelling the rosewater her mother used in her hair, letting the familiar scent calm her. "I didn't turn Billy Stoughton into a cockroach today," she whispered.

She heard the muffled giggle from her mother. "Well, that's good," her mother whispered back. "Because I'd hate to have to tell Mrs. Stoughton that her son was a cockroach. Although it might have been an improvement."

Agnes giggled too, then sighed. "Why are people mean?" she asked, her voice slightly quivering.

"I don't know, sweetheart," her mother replied sadly. "All I know is that we can't let what they do change who we are."

Agnes leaned back, her face filled with confusion as she faced her mother. "We just let them be mean to us, and we don't do anything about it?" she asked incredulously.

Her mother lifted her hand and cradled her daughter's cheek. "It's so hard," she agreed. "Especially when it would be so easy to justify our actions because they were mean to us first, right?"

Agnes nodded, her eyes wide. "Right," she said earnestly.

"But what do we know?" her mother asked. "What is our rule?"

Agnes inhaled deeply and released it slowly. "An harm it none," she finally replied with exasperation. "Even if they're idiots, an harm it none."

Her mother nodded and bit back her smile. "Exactly, my brilliant little witch," she said softly, leaning forward and placing a kiss on her daughter's forehead. "Even if they're idiots."

Chapter Two

(Current day)

"Idiots!!! They are all idiots!!!" Hazel exclaimed as she stormed into the kitchen.

Agnes looked up from the bottles of Elderberry Syrup she was filling, gazed at her youngest daughter, and bit back a smile. Then she looked back down to the amber bottles before her, straightened the funnel on the next bottle to be used, and shook her head. "Who are idiots?" she asked mildly.

"Everyone," Hazel sighed with frustration as she slipped into a tall chair on the opposite side of the counter as her mother. She reached over to a platter filled with muffins and selected a blueberry one with streusel topping. She began to methodically peel the wrapper away from the muffin while her mother waited patiently, ladling the warm, dark syrup into the amber bottle.

Hazel took a nibble of the streusel and sighed again. "Okay, I'm ready to talk," she admitted.

Agnes moved the metal funnel to the next sterilized bottle and then sealed the filled one with a cap. "Okay, I'm ready to listen," she replied.

"I've contacted all of the covens in the Midwest," she paused and shook her head. "And none of them are willing to help."

"Did they say why?" Agnes said, her hand shaking slightly as she scooped up more of the syrup.

"It's not our fight," Hazel said, taking an angry bite out of the muffin. Then, with her mouth full, she added, "Whose fight is it? I mean, if the demon wins, the world as we know it is pretty much over."

"Did you mention that to them," Agnes asked, her heart dropping, but her smile pasted in place.

Hazel nodded sadly. "Yeah, I did," she said. "In no uncertain terms, and they still refused to help. They're nothing but cowards."

Agnes capped the last bottle and placed the funnel into the empty pot before carrying them both to the large farmer's sink. "Fear is a common reaction to the

11

unknown," she said, turning on the water to rinse out the pot. "And, unfortunately, in this day and age, people tend to let fear rule their decisions."

"So, what are we going to do?" Hazel asked.

"Do about what?" Cat asked, coming in through the back door. She looked at the bottles on the counter and smiled. "Oh, good, now that flu season is approaching, we've been getting requests for Elderberry Syrup." She assessed the amber bottles lining the counter and turned to her mother. "Can you make another four batches, just like this?"

Agnes pulled a cotton dishtowel from the rack and dried her large stainless-steel pot and nodded. "Sure, just let me…"

"How can you both be talking about Elderberry Syrup when we only have a few more days before the potential end of the world happens?" Hazel interrupted.

Cat turned to her sister. "What did I miss?" she asked.

"None of the covens are going to help us," Hazel said. "Once again, we're on our own."

Cat sighed softly. "Well, disappointed, but not surprising," she said. "Our family has been on our own for decades. I guess that's why we were chosen, we're the only ones who would follow through."

"It sucks," Hazel said, her eyes filling with tears. "It totally sucks."

Cat placed her arm around Hazel's shoulders and hugged her. "Yes, it does," she said. "But, if we were chosen, it means there's a way to win."

Hazel dashed away her tears and rolled her eyes. "Oh, sure, now that you and Donovan are together, the whole world is sunshine and lollipops," she replied. "But what if...what if because of the changes that occurred after the spell happened, we aren't enough? What if three from one doesn't work anymore? What if things are so screwed up that we are basically walking to our deaths on Samhain?"

Agnes leaned on the counter across from Hazel and met her daughter's eyes. "Where is all of this coming from?" she asked, concern wrinkling her brow. "Have you received a vision?"

Sighing, Hazel laid her hands protectively on her swollen belly and shook her head. Her eyes once again filled with tears. "I can't take any chances," she whispered, her voice filled with emotion. "We need to win."

Cat placed her hand over her sister's and nodded. "You're right," she agreed. "We need to win, and we need to be sure we have all the information we can get. Let's cast a circle tonight and see how much more information we can get from the original three."

Chapter Three

A few hours later, Agnes stepped outside onto the back deck, closed her eyes, and inhaled the crisp, cool air of autumn.

"You look the same as you did when I met you at the Autumnal Equinox Ritual so many years ago," Finias said, his low voice a soothing balm to her troubled heart.

She opened her eyes and smiled at him. "I remember watching you walk through the grove of oak trees like you were the Green Man himself," she replied softly, love shining from her eyes.

He grinned at her. "Well, perhaps the Brown Man, my sweet," he teased, stepping up and holding his hand out to her. She placed her hand in his, climbed down the steps, and stood before him. He tenderly stroked her cheek and then cradled her head in his hands. "The perfect equinox meeting. The perfect equilibrium when day and night were equally matched."

He bent forward and placed a kiss on her forehead. "And light and dark were drawn to each other, equal, but different," he whispered, placing a kiss on her cheek. "And finally, the perfect match between male and female."

He pulled her to him and covered her lips with his own.

She trembled in his arms, aware of not only his hunger but also her answering need. It had been like this from the beginning, two hearts, two souls perfectly matched.

"You were always," he murmured as if he had read her mind, "always my perfect match. The other part of me."

She reached up and slipped her arms around his neck, drawing him back to her. "You were always," she said softly, "my one true love. My only match."

He smiled at her and kissed her again. "And you mine," he said.

The sound of a car pulling into the driveway drew their attention away from each other, and they stepped back to see who was arriving. Cat's vehicle drove down the dirt lane and pulled up next to the porch. She smiled at them as she got out of the car. "Catching up?" she asked with a saucy smile.

"You didn't teach our daughter much tact," Finias replied with a wink.

"And I didn't teach her about good timing either," Agnes quipped.

Cat hurried over to them and enfolded them both in a hug. "I got what you needed for dinner tonight," she told Agnes. "And I told everyone about casting the circle."

"Is everyone coming?" Agnes asked.

"Wouldn't miss it for the world," Cat replied, and then she smiled at her father. "So, how's it going having all of the dads staying with you at the B&B?"

Finias chuckled. "Well, not as badly as you would think," he said. "We have all agreed not to argue about which daughter is the most beautiful and intelligent. But, of course, we all know that my daughter is."

Cat laughed and reached up to kiss him on his cheek. "And my father is the wisest," she teased. "As well as the most clairvoyant. Renting all three rooms at the B&B was inspired."

He smiled at her. "Well, you know, I might have a little advantage in that area."

"Nothing like being able to see visions to give a man an advantage," she agreed.

"Yes, nothing like…" he suddenly stopped speaking, as his eyes widened, and he stared, unfocused, at the sky. A moment later, he shook his head and looked at the two women who were staring at him.

"What happened?" Cat asked.

Finias smiled at his daughter and shrugged. "Just a passing thought," he said mildly, then he squeezed Agnes' hand and looked down at her. "So, are we still going on the walk you promised me?"

"Walk?" she questioned, then she nodded in understanding. "Well, of course, we're going on our walk. I have plenty of time before I have to make dinner."

Agnes turned to Cat. "If you don't mind putting the groceries away," she requested, "we shouldn't be long at all."

Cat stared pointedly at her parents and shook her head. "I'm not so obtuse that I don't see that something's going on here," she said. "But I respect your privacy, as long as you're not trying to protect us from anything. We are not children. And the more we understand, the more we can be prepared."

Finias leaned over and kissed Cat on her forehead. "I never thought you were obtuse," he said. "And you're right, there is something I need to discuss with your mother before we cast the circle. And, when the time is right, we will share it with you."

Cat nodded. "Fair enough."

Agnes linked her arm through Finias' arm. "I'll show you my favorite place to think," she explained.

19

"I would love that," he replied, then he glanced around. "No Fuzzy to chaperone us?"

Smiling, Agnes shook her head. "No, Fuzzy has decided that he needs to watch over Hazel," she said. "Which is driving Hazel a little crazy because he's always in her way."

"I think it's adorable," Cat said, pulling bags out of the back seat of her vehicle. "Fuzzy has always been in tune with all of us, and he must sense that Hazel is feeling more vulnerable than the rest of us."

"She is more vulnerable," Agnes replied. "She has to think about the child growing inside of her, too, not just herself."

Cat's eyes softened, and she nodded. "She's going to make an amazing mom," she said.

"And you're going to be an amazing aunt," Agnes added. "Now, go inside and get ready for tonight. We'll be back soon. "

Chapter Four

"This isn't good," Professor Henry McDermott muttered as he studied the information in an ancient leather-bound book. "This is not good at all."

Rowan Willoughby looked up from her microscope and pushed her glasses up on her nose. "What?" she asked. "What's not good?"

Henry lifted his head and met her eyes. "If what I'm reading here is correct, we are not just dealing with any demon, we are dealing with Belial," he said, his voice low and concerned. "And according to the *Pseudomonarchia Daemonum*, he has 80 legions of demons at his behest."

Rowan stepped away from the stainless-steel table and walked over to where Henry was sitting at the desk. "Okay, two questions," she said, pulling up a chair next to him. "First, what is the pseudo-whatchamacallit, and, second, how many are in a legion?"

Henry nodded slowly and ran his hand through his hair, a sight that usually endeared him even more to Rowan, but the somberness in his eyes caused her stomach to tighten.

"The *Pseudomonarchia Daemonum* was initially just an appendix to a grimoire written in 1577. It was basically a list of demons and their characteristics," he explained. "There are sixty-nine demons listed in the book. Our guy, Belial, is number sixty-eight with number sixty-nine being Lucifer."

Rowan exhaled slowly. "Okay, wow, that's not good news," she said.

"And now for even worse news," Henry added. "A legion of demons is equal to 6,666 demons."

"Well, of course, it is," she replied, her heart pounding and her voice shaking. "And how are we supposed to deal with that?"

Henry turned in his chair and took her hands in his. He leaned forward and placed a comforting kiss on her forehead. "Well, you know," he said wryly, "Samhain is a holiday, so maybe a lot of them will be out of town."

A burst of surprised laughter spilled from her lips before she could stop it, but it didn't stop the fear in her heart. She laid her head against his chest and sighed. "Sure, that's probably the case," she breathed. "And then what? Even with the extra dads thrown in, there's only ten of us. We each get eight legions?"

Henry wrapped his arms around her and held her tightly. "Maybe they can't interfere because of the conditions of the spell," Henry suggested, laying his head against hers. "Maybe they are bound, and only Belial can confront us."

"Which is not too comforting either," Rowan inserted, lifting her head and meeting his eyes.

"But remember, we've been dealing with this same demon all along," he insisted. "And we've been winning."

"Yes, but the demon has not been up to full power yet," she reminded him. "On Samhain, he will have all of

23

his power available to him and the power of those he has under his control."

He slid his hands to her shoulders and held her firmly. "We need to have faith, Rowan," he said with conviction. "We need to believe that we can win. We need to believe that good will be able to overcome evil. We need to be sure, in our hearts, that we can stand up to it."

"Even if it's the last thing we do?" she asked softly.

"If it's the last thing we do," he replied, laying his forehead against hers. "Then, we will do it together, and I will meet you on the other side, knowing that we did all we could to stop him."

"Why does death sound so noble when you talk about it?" she teased.

He grinned at her and planted a quick kiss on her lips. "It's my British accent," he replied. "It makes everything sound noble."

"I love you, Professor Henry McDermott," she whispered urgently. "And I would really like to live to a ripe old age with you by my side."

He threaded his hand through her hair, and she leaned her cheek against his palm. "I adore you, Rowan Willoughby," he said tenderly. "And I want you to become the mother of my children. I want to watch them grow and thrive, surrounded by love and security. I don't want them to be burdened by the threat of a curse in their lifetime."

She nodded. "We need to end this," she agreed. "But it's going to take all of us."

He kissed her again, lingering to make sure he committed her taste, her scent, and the passion she stirred inside of him to his memory. He would never admit it, but the idea of facing eighty legions of demons shook him to the core.

"We need to bring this to the circle tonight," he said, as he gently broke off the kiss.

She kissed him once more, committing his touch to her own memory. "In the meantime, you keep studying those manuscripts, my dear, darling professor, and figure out the best way to send Belial back to hell."

Chapter Five

The steep climb up to the top of the ridge was done in companionable silence. Agnes walked in front, navigating the path and the low-hanging branches that were now filled with leaves of gold, amber, red, and brown. The scent of pine, from the conifers on the top of the ridge, wafted down the trail, carried by a gentle autumn breeze. The sun, which was just beginning to settle behind the ridge, illuminated the valley below in a flourish of red-gold warmth. Agnes paused at a widening of the path and looked out over the beauty before her.

"It's hard to believe that we can live in a world with such beauty and tranquility on the one hand," Finias said, coming up behind her, "and such evil and discord on the other."

She nodded, still staring at the scene before her. "But this…" she whispered. "This is part of what we are fighting for."

"Yes," he agreed. "So that our children and our grandchildren can one day stand here and delight in the wonder below."

She turned and looked up at him. "Will you think less of me if I admit that I'm terrified?" she asked.

He smiled at her and shook his head. "I believe that being terrified means you have a good grasp on the situation before us," he said. "Only a fool would think that this is going to be easy."

She turned back to the scene before them. "And my momma didn't raise no fool," she said quietly, with a sad smile.

He placed his hands on her shoulders and leaned forward, his face next to her ear. "As I recall," he whispered. "Your mother raised a warrior."

Unbidden, a memory came to mind.

"I don't want to go to school," Agnes said *defiantly, crossing her eight-year-old arms over her chest. "I don't want to go, and you can't make me."*

28

Her mother nodded serenely and knelt down in front of her daughter. She saw not only the defiance but the fear and sadness behind her daughter's words. It was not easy to be a Willoughby, but it was not going to get any easier as she got older. She would need to learn courage now, in her youth.

She leaned forward, touched her forehead to her daughter's forehead, and sighed softly. "I understand," she said gently. "It's hard to have to deal with ignorance and meanness every day, isn't it?"

Tiny tears splashed out of green eyes, and she felt her daughter shudder. "It's so hard, mom," she admitted. "It's just so hard. Ben Stoughton teases me every day. He calls me names, he pushes me down, and the other kids laugh at me."

Placing her arms around her daughter, she hugged her and held her in her arms. "Yes, I know," she said. "It happened to me too, when I was your age. Some people can be very cruel."

29

There was a moment of silence, a pause to consider her mother's words. "It happened to you too?" Agnes asked, her voice filled with bewilderment.

Her mother nodded slowly. "Yes, it wasn't Ben Stoughton, but someone just like him," she replied. "I suppose there will always be people like Ben Stoughton in the world. He didn't like me because he was afraid of me, and he didn't like to feel that way."

"Why was he afraid of you?"

"Well, because the Willoughbys have never been afraid to do the right thing," she said. "They have never been afraid to stand up for those who were weaker than they. They have always stood for 'an harm in none' and led their lives in a way that exemplified that."

"Why would that make him afraid?" Agnes asked.

"People are often afraid of what they don't understand," she explained. "When you are raised to bully, to take advantage of others, and to not care about those around you – facing someone like us creates confusion and fear."

30

"He's afraid of me," the little girl whispered slowly. Then she paused for another moment. "And what did you do? Did you stop going to school?"

Her mother chose her words carefully. "No, I continued to go to school," she finally said, "for several reasons. One, I didn't want him to think he could bully me. I didn't want him to believe he had won." She chuckled softly. "I believe that was more pride than wisdom. But then, there were the others."

"The others?" Agnes asked, pulling back and meeting her mother's eyes.

"The others who were not as strong as I was," she explained. "The others who would end up being victims to the bullies if I wasn't there. The others who would follow along with the meanness unless I showed them an alternative. The others who just needed a good example."

Agnes nodded slowly. "I'm going to go to school today," she decided, her voice calm but firm. "Because I'm a Willoughby."

31

Pulling her daughter back into her arms for another hug, her mother kissed the top of her head and whispered. "Yes, darling, because you're a Willoughby."

"My whole life, I was raised to understand that this was my destiny," Agnes said to Finias as the memory ended, "and the destiny of my daughters. But now…"

"Now you want to protect them," he said. "You want them to be safe."

She nodded. "Why should they have to risk their lives and die so others will be safe?"

Finias sighed. "That is a very old and complex question, is it not?" he asked. "Why should one, who is not deserving of the penalty, have to pay the price for so many who are not deserving of the prize?"

"What's the answer?" she asked.

"It's easy and it's complex all at the same time. Love," he replied with a sad sigh. "Love for all mankind was the reason behind the greatest sacrifice. Love for their fellow countrymen is the reason for those who serve in our military. Love for their communities is the reason for first responders. Love can be a powerful motivation."

Without responding, Agnes moved away from the ledge and continued back up the path to the top of the ridge. When she reached the top, she stopped to take a deep breath and study this space that was her favorite getaway. The narrow path opened to a grassy knoll that offered a 360-degree view of the valley and surrounding countryside. Walking to the top of the knoll, she stopped, her long auburn hair blowing in the wind, and raised her hands to the sky.

"You look like a goddess," Finias said, joining her. He slipped his arms around her waist and pulled her against him, then lowered his lips to hers and kissed her with an urgency she hadn't felt in a long time. She slipped her arms around his neck and returned his kiss. All her emotions—fear, passion, uncertainty, and love—melding into it. They stayed clasped in each other's arms for several minutes, and then they slowly stepped apart, their breath unsteady, and their eyes filled with a tumult of emotion.

Agnes inhaled deeply and then closed her eyes for a moment, breaking their connection. Finally, she opened her eyes, and instead of the passion that filled them a moment earlier, they were calm and composed. "You needed to speak to me," she said, trying to keep her voice from trembling. "What did you see?"

He too closed his eyes, reigning in his passions, controlling his feelings for the woman before him. When he opened them, he too was composed, but there were still lingering flames of desire in them. "I saw legions," he said.

A chill entered her heart and shook her to her core. "Legions?" she asked.

"I saw a granite stone with a large fissure," he said. "We were there, all of us. The fissure widened, and there were flames. From the flames came the demon, and behind him were legions of others of his kind."

Her heart pounded in her chest. She drew a deep, shuddering breath. "How many?"

"Too many to count," he replied. He paused for a long moment and then met her eyes. "Too many to fight."

She nodded wordlessly and wrapped her arms around her chest. "I've seen it too," she admitted. "But I was hoping I was wrong."

She turned and stared out over the woods, down to where her home lay, surrounded by farmland. She could see Hazel walking from the barn to the house with Fuzzy walking alongside her, nearly tripping her because he was so close. Then Joseph jogged down the back steps and over to her, catching her up in his arms and kissing her thoroughly.

She watched Rowan and Henry walk out of the Still Room chatting with each other and holding hands.

She watched Donovan pull his car into the drive and park, and Cat run out of the house and throw herself into his awaiting arms.

Her daughters and their men. They had a right to more than a futile war and a brief life. They had a right to happiness, to children, to a future.

She turned back to Finias and nodded. "Okay, if there are too many to fight, what can we do to even the odds?" she asked, the fire back in her eyes.

He nodded in approval and smiled. "See, there's the warrior."

Chapter Six

Wanda Wildes parked her car in the small parking area on the street in front of the Iron Mountain Prison. She stepped out of the car, her tall, black high heels clicking against the asphalt, and then straightened her barely-there leather skirt. She arranged her red silk blouse to accentuate her cleavage and then reached into her purse for a small, amber vial that was closed with a cork. Pulling the cork from the top, she could immediately smell the combination of herbs and oils that made up the love-philter. She dabbed the liquid onto the sensitive spots behind her ears, on her wrists, and from the base of her neck down to the beginning of her cleavage. Then she inhaled deeply and smiled with satisfaction. She could already feel her body warming, sending out pheromones into the surrounding air.

Closing the vial, she slipped it back into her purse and stepped up to the sidewalk, making her way up the stone stairs and through the doors of the jail. She walked to the counter and smiled at the officer across from her. Leaning forward, displaying an ample amount of cleavage, and sending the scent of the philter in his direction, she smiled sweetly.

"I'm wondering if you can help me," she said, her voice soft and low. "I'm here to visit my father, Wade Wildes."

The officer closed the file drawer he'd been glancing through and turned, his face one of boredom and contempt. "You got a daddy here?" he asked contemptuously. "What kind of daddy wants his daughter to come to a place like this?"

She leaned further against the counter and conjured a bit of wind to carry her scent to the officer. "Well, he's not crazy about me visiting him," she admitted, bending her head and gazing at him through lowered eyelashes. "But I get so lonely."

Suddenly, the officer shook his head and cleared his throat. He handed her a small clipboard with a form attached to it and a pencil. "Fill out this information," he said, his voice tight. "And I'll need to see some form of I.D."

She reached out and brushed her hand against his as she took the clipboard from him. His hand shook, and she smiled slowly. "Of course, officer," she whispered.

She began to fill out the form, occasionally glancing at the officer who was loosening his tie and patting his forehead with a tissue. She conjured up another breeze, sending more of the scent in the officer's direction as she handed the clipboard back to him, along with her drivers' license. "Will I need to be frisked?" she asked, running her tongue slowly over her upper lip as she met his eyes.

He swallowed audibly and nodded. "Yes. Yes, ma'am," he stammered. "I'll call down and get one of the female guards to assist in that."

She laid her hand over his and stroked it slowly. "I don't think that's necessary," she said with a wry smile. "I'd feel much more comfortable having you take care of the job."

"I'm sorry," he replied, shaking his head, sweat pooling on his forehead and his upper lip. "That's against regulations."

She stepped back and unbuttoned the top two buttons of her blouse, exposing a lacy black bra. "Wouldn't you rather bend the rules today?" she asked. "I think it could be an enjoyable experience for both of us."

He nodded slowly, his eyes wide and unblinking. "Enjoyable," he repeated.

She smiled and nodded. "I feel so much safer when I'm in the hands of the law," she teased.

"Yes, ma'am," he choked. "If you will step this way."

She sauntered around the counter, and he pressed the buzzer to open the gate and let her through. She stepped up to him and smiled. "Thank you for your dedication to the job," she whispered, sliding a finger from between her breasts across her collarbone.

He cleared his throat. "Yes, ma'am," he gasped.

He led her to a small room situated next to the guard station. The walls were cinderblock, the metal table and chair were bolted to the floor, and a small barred window twelve feet up in the wall provided the only natural light. She slipped onto the table and leaned backwards. "I'm ready when you are," she encouraged.

He cleared his throat again and nodded. "I need to…I need to call for someone to cover the desk," he replied.

"Why don't you just lock the front door?" she suggested. "Then we won't be disturbed."

He shook his head. "I could lose my job…" he started.

She unbuttoned another button. "You could," she replied. "But, I promise it will be worth it."

He left her for a moment, and she could hear him rushing out to the entrance area and locking the door. She quickly retrieved the vial, and this time generously applied the potion to her body.

She had just slipped the vial back in her purse when he came back, closed the door, and locked it. "I need to check your purse first," he announced.

She nodded and held it up towards him. He stepped forward and inhaled. "What is that…" he began.

She bent forward and ran her hand slowly up his chest. "I feel it too," she breathed, closing her eyes and gasping softly. "What are you doing to me? I need you. I need you now!"

He grabbed her upper arms and pulled her to him, sliding her forward on the table. His labored breathing was music to her ears. She bit back her laughter as he fumbled with his own clothing and nearly shouted for joy when she heard the sound of her purse hitting the floor beneath the table.

Chapter Seven

Straightening her skirt and tucking in her blouse, she smiled at the officer splayed out on the chair, a look of astonishment on his face. "I'll just go visit my father now," she said with a grin. "Don't get up, I know the way."

She reached down and picked up her purse, slung it over her shoulder, and smiled at him again. "Have a nice day, officer," she trilled with a quick wave and closed the door behind her.

Walking over to the counter, she filled in the pass, signed the officer's name, and pressed the button to allow her to enter the inside of the prison. With her heels clicking against the linoleum tile on the floors, she made her way purposefully to the visitor's area in the back of the prison. Reaching the metal door with the reinforced glass window, she held her pass up to the guard on the other side. He nodded and unlocked the door, pointing her to the table across the room where her father sat.

She smiled sweetly at him and sauntered across the room to sit in the plastic chair across from her father.

"Took your sweet time coming," Wade Wildes growled. He was past middle-aged, his complexion was pasty, his eyes red-rimmed, and his hair thin and scraggly. A former cop, even a crooked former cop, did not have an easy life inside the confines of a prison.

Wanda lifted her purse onto the table and glared at him. "You should be thanking me," she replied angrily.

"Did you bring it," he whispered harshly, ignoring her comment.

She sighed, turning her purse on its side and reaching in. "Of course, I did," she said, carefully sliding a packet from her purse onto the table top.

Wade reached over and placed his hands over hers. "It's so good to see you, darling," he said loudly. "But, I really don't like you making these trips to see me."

She slid the twelve-inch long, narrow package into his sleeve and smiled back. "But Daddy, you know how much I miss you," she replied.

Wade nodded. "You've got a big, fat hickey on your neck," he said, pointing to the large bruise near her collarbone. "That guard going to remember anything?"

She sighed, conjured a quick healing spell to make the discoloration disappear, and then shook her head. "He inhaled so much philter that he's going to be making passes at the streetlights when he drives home tonight," she answered. "And tomorrow morning, he's going to wake up with the world's worst headache."

"That's my girl," Wade replied with a nasty smile, and then the smile disappeared. "What's going on with them Willoughbys?"

"There's more of them," she said softly. "And we don't have much time."

He nodded, his face filled with hate. "Yeah, and thanks to you," he whispered. "We'll be out of here by the end of the day."

Two other men approached the table and sat down on either side of her father. Neal Abbott, her father's old partner, and Ben Stoughton, the former chief of police.

"Wanda," Ben said, nodding easily. "Good to see you."

"And you, sir," she replied, straightening in her chair and surreptitiously wiping the moisture from her palms on her skirt. The former leader of their coven was not a man to cross; she had seen more than one life ruined because Ben Stoughton decided he didn't like them.

"So, you brought your daddy a little gift?" he asked, his flint-steel eyes boring into hers.

She shivered slightly and then nodded. "Yes. Yes, the gift has been delivered," she replied softly.

"And it's exactly what I wanted?" he asked, his voice low and menacing.

She nodded. "Yes, I followed your instructions exactly," she whispered, her voice trembling.

Ben sat back and nodded his approval, then he reached over and slapped Neal's back with enough force to nearly knock him off his chair. "Your nephew better take back those comments he made about Wade's girl here," he said, leaning down and glancing past her father to Neal. "She's a whole lot more than just a blonde bimbo."

"He said that?" Wanda exclaimed quietly. She turned to Neal. "Buck said that about me?"

Ben grinned and sat back, satisfied to watch the tempest he'd stirred up.

"Wanda, honey, he didn't mean nothing by it," Neal replied. "You know Buck, always shooting off his mouth."

Her eyes narrowed, and she pursed her lips. "Well, maybe your nephew is gonna have to find his own ride back to Whitewater," she whispered fiercely. "Maybe I don't…"

The words caught in her mouth as she felt a tightening pressure around her throat. She wheezed and fought for air. Then she turned to look at Ben, whose face was taut and eyes menacing. "No one is going to mess with my plan, do you understand?" he growled quietly.

She nodded as tears streamed down her face, and the room started to darken.

"Good," he replied, and she felt the pressure from around her neck release.

She gulped in air and trembled with fear.

"You be outside, ready, tonight," he said quietly. "You have the car running and the doors unlocked. You have your license plate covered with mud, so the cameras can't pick it up. You got that?"

She nodded wordlessly.

Ben stood up, leaned over, and placed a quick kiss on her head. "Now you go home and be safe, little one," he said loudly, his voice carrying across the room. "Thanks for visiting. Come on, boys."

Wade and Neal stumbled out of their chairs and immediately followed Ben out of the room. Wanda took another deep breath, calmed herself, and then turned to the nearest guard.

"I'm done here," she said, standing up and walked to the locked door.

The guard smiled at her and nodded. "You take care, you hear?"

She paused for a moment and looked at his nametag, Kipling.

"You too, Officer Kipling," she whispered. "You too."

Chapter Eight

Dinner was a joyful and raucous event with conversations going in all different directions around the large table. The food was delicious and abundant. Agnes felt that a feast needed to be shared before the ceremony of casting the circle, and she did her best to provide the feast. She sat at the head of the table, looking around at her family, her heart troubled with fears that nothing they could do would be enough.

She felt a warm hand over hers, and a reassuring squeeze brought her attention back to the man at her side.

"You should be proud," Finias whispered to her. "You have an amazing family."

She smiled at him and nodded. "I was just thinking that a few short months ago, it was only the four of us," she said. "Now, each of my daughters have found their soulmates, as well as been introduced to their fathers. Quite a change."

"A necessary change, I would say," he agreed. "And one in which fate played no small part."

"I can only hope that fate will be kind to us," she said, lowering her voice.

"I believe that fate is neither kind or unkind, it just sets in motions the things that need to be," he replied softly and then squeezed her hand again. "And we will be ready for whatever that is."

She sighed and nodded again. "Yes," she agreed. "Yes, we will."

On the left side of the table, Rowan leaned back in her chair as Henry and her father, Seamus Galway, a college professor from Trinity College in Dublin, discussed their respective rugby teams' age-old rivalry. They were seated on either side of her, and, as the conversation heated, she felt moving out of the line of fire was in her own best interests.

"Aye, it was a close one," Seamus said, his blue eyes sparkling with mischief. "If you call a total pounding close."

Henry chuckled and nodded. "Well, Seamus, as you are an ancient history professor at Trinity College, I understand why you only point to past years and not the current one," he acknowledged. "But this year, you sent your wee lassies out to play instead of your rugby team."

Seamus laughed and acknowledged the hit. "Well, truly, we only thought it fair to your team that we sent out the lassies," he teased. "Seeing as the boys wiped the field with your English aristocrats with no problem. Perhaps they ought to try chugging a good draft instead of a cup of tea."

Henry laughed too and nodded. "Perhaps they should, indeed," he agreed.

"Okay," Rowan said, sitting forward in her seat and blocking their view of each other. "I think it's time to put rugby to the side and talk of other things." She looked pointedly at each of the men. "More pleasant things."

"Of course. Of course. Of course," Seamus soothed, and then he winked at Henry around his daughter. "Should we try politics for a turn?"

Rowan threw herself back in her chair and shook her head. "I give up," she moaned dramatically. "I just give up."

Across from them, Hazel was involved in a totally different kind of conversation with her father, Dustin Carter, an aerospace engineer and avid outdoorsman, and her fiancé Joseph.

"No, dad, it's not scientific, it's magic," Hazel argued.

"But even magic has scientific roots," Dustin replied. "And that's what is so amazing about it." He turned to Joseph. "If we could understand the basic premise behind the stealth ability of your village, we could use that basic concept as we engineer fighter planes."

Joseph studied his soon-to-be father-in-law for a moment and then slowly shook his head. "What happens to an harm it none?" he asked.

Dustin was taken aback for a moment, then he nodded. "I was initially going to say that we would only use it for good," he replied with a look of chagrin. "But then I realized that once the technology is out there, I couldn't guarantee who would use it and for what causes."

"That's one of the problems we face in the world today," Joseph said. "And I'm speaking as a law enforcement officer, not someone who can use magic. So many people, so many leaders, lack basic integrity. They have been caught up in the power and fortune of their positions and have lost the concept that they were put in that position to serve, not rule."

Dustin nodded slowly. "I agree," he said. "It's unfortunate that as we build and create, we also have to look at how the technology could potentially be used to hurt mankind rather than just how it could be used to help."

"You are both making me nervous about giving birth to our baby," Hazel interrupted. "Can't we talk about something else, like cures for cancer or the rising economy or…"

Suddenly there was a lull in the conversation, a brief moment of silence, and Henry's voice seemed to echo in the room.

"Demons."

He quickly glanced around the table and closed his eyes in regret. "I'm so sorry," he apologized. "I didn't mean…"

"It needed to be said," Finias inserted. "It's a conversation that we should have before we cast the circle."

Hazel looked across at Henry and sighed "That was not what I had in mind when I wanted to change the subject," she accused gently.

Henry nodded sadly. "I'm sorry," he replied. "And I'm afraid what I have to suggest isn't going to brighten anyone's day."

Chapter Nine

"Belial?" Donovan asked. "Are you sure?"

"Well, as sure as I can be with the information available to me," Henry replied. "But you've had the most experience with the demon, what do you think?"

Donovan nodded slowly and glanced at Cat with a sorrowful expression on his face. "Knowing how powerful he was, even when he was still under the charm," he began. "And then, seeing the influence he had on the other coven…" He nodded. "Yes, I could see that it could be Belial."

"Eighty legions of demons following him?" Hazel asked, astonished.

Henry shrugged. "Well, that was according to Johann Weyer in the *Pseudomonarchia Daemonum*. But *The Goetia,* written by S.L. MacGregor Mathers, states that he only governs fifty legions."

"Never trust those Scots," Seamus muttered. "Always playing with numbers."

Hazel leaned back in her chair, her eyes wide with concern, and inhaled deeply. "Okay, well then, only fifty legions," she said slowly. "That's much better."

"Well, it's 333,300 demons compared to 533,280 demons," Henry replied. "So, that's a difference of 199,980 demons."

"Oh, piece of cake," Hazel grumbled. "Only 333,000 demons."

"And there's ten of us," Joseph said, shaking his head. "So, that would either leave each of us with 33,000 to fight or 53,000 to fight." He turned to Agnes. "This can't be what the sisters intended. They already made the ultimate sacrifice; it wasn't supposed to be like this."

"You're right," Agnes replied. "Initially, we thought that this was supposed to be a meeting of the three against the demon. Then, as we were able to use Henry's ancestor's grimoire, we learned that the three needed to find their soulmates in order to win against this evil. But now, I feel like everything is up in the air. The sisters didn't realize that the followers of the Pratt Institute of

57

Spiritualism would be fooled by a member of the Wildes Coven. We were able to destroy the amulet but could not reverse the spell."

"Is there any point in trying to reverse the spell now?" Donovan asked. "Perhaps we could convince Wanda to work on our side."

"If that happens, we don't have to worry about the demon," Hazel inserted. "Because hell will have frozen over, and he won't be able to get out anyway."

Joseph put his arm around Hazel's shoulders and hugged her. "You know, she could see the error of her ways and change," he suggested.

Hazel looked up at him and shook her head. "She's got generations of mean girl inside of her," she argued. "I don't see it happening."

"Actually, it's a moot point," Henry inserted. "The damage was done by the spell one hundred years ago. Unless we can go back in time, we can't undo the harm that's already been done."

"What else do you know about this demon?" Dustin asked. "Do we know its weaknesses? Do we know some of its characteristics?"

"According to the ancient writings, he can be constrained by divine power," Henry said. "He is dedicated to creating wickedness and guilt in humankind. He is the personification of lies and evil. Pride was his downfall. He had actually been captured in a vessel and thrown into a lake, but someone, thinking the vessel contained treasure, broke it open and released him."

"And, in his weakened state, we've been able to defeat him," Donovan added.

"But how different will he be without the constraints of the spell?" Cat asked. "Will his power be doubled or tripled?"

"And how do we fight legions?" Rowan asked. "Do we concentrate on the demon, and once he's defeated, the legions will go away?"

"Those are all very good questions," Agnes said. "And I believe our first source for information needs to be

59

the three. So, if everyone is ready, we can clean things up

here and cast the circle."

Chapter Ten

The table was quickly cleared, and the large rug that covered the inlaid Celtic quaternary knot was moved to the side of the room. The Willoughby women stood on one of the outer points of the interconnected ovals that created the circle, and the men stood inside facing them.

The air in the room was suddenly filled with power, like the air during a lightning storm. Agnes could feel the power encompassing them even before she began the ritual. She looked at each of her daughters as they stood, power lifting the ends of their hair into the air, intensifying the glow from their eyes, and radiating from their skin.

"Are you ready?" Agnes asked, and her daughters all nodded their heads in acquiescence.

Lifting her smudge stick above her head, Agnes began the ceremony. Like an artist with a brush, the wisp of smoke from the smudge stick trailed a line in the air above her and then down in front of her body. "I cleanse the space to the east," she chanted slowly.

Catalpa lifted her smudge stick and met Donovan's eyes for just a moment. Then she drew it above her head and down in front of her body. "I cleanse the space to the south."

Hazel, in the next space, lifted her smudge stick with one hand, while resting her other hand protectively on her belly. "I cleanse the space to the west," she said softly, moving the stick horizontally, then vertically mimicking her mother and sister.

Finally, Rowan repeated the same actions and chanted, "I cleanse the space to the north."

When she was done, all the women turned and walked clockwise around the edge of the circle, their arms outstretched, and a trail of soft grey sage smoke surrounding them.

"We cleanse all spaces in between," they chanted in unison.

When they arrived back in their beginning

positions, they raised their arms above their heads, then

stretched them outwards, so the distance between them

from fingertip to fingertip was about twelve inches. The

energy in the circle had intensified, and static electricity

was causing their hair to rise and circle their heads like

halos.

"We cast this circle, as is our right," Agnes

commanded, her voice strong and clear. "To protect us

with thy holy light. Nothing can harm or corrupt our plea.

As we ask, so mote it be."

Golden light appeared above Agnes and traveled

down through the top of her head into her arms. Then it

cascaded from mother to daughters, from arm to arm, until

the entire circle was surrounded by the protection of the

light.

Agnes took a deep breath and glanced over to her

daughters, one by one. "Well done," she whispered. "We

are safe within our circle."

Finias came forward, took Agnes' hand, and led her to an embroidered pillow inside the circle. She sat down, and he sat next to her.

"What shall we do first?" he asked.

"I think we should use Henry's Grimoire to help summon the sisters," she suggested. She turned to Cat, who was just sitting down. "Do you have it?"

Cat nodded and slipped the grimoire out from underneath her pillow. "Yes, I thought we might need it tonight," she said.

She laid the book on the floor and opened up the cover, then she turned to Henry. "Since this is from your family," she said, "you probably ought to do the honors."

Henry nodded slowly. "Okay, but remember, I might need your help," he said with a little chagrin. "Poems, or spells, don't seem to be my forte."

He knelt in front of the book and closed his eyes.

As we journey towards our fate

We plead unto the three

For guidance to corroborate

Our path, so mote it be.

Henry opened his eyes and glanced at Rowan, who smiled at him and nodded encouragingly. "Well done," she mouthed.

Suddenly the ceiling above them seemed to peel back, opening up a portal to another world. Three women, all dressed in white, stood at the entrance to the portal and looked down on the group.

"Well done indeed," one of the women said, smiling at Henry. "You have learned much in a short time. Patience is proud of you."

"Is Patience okay?" Rowan asked.

The woman turned to Rowan and nodded. "Yes, she is fine. And she sends her love."

Then the woman looked at Agnes. "The way has changed, has it not?"

Agnes nodded. "Yes, none of us were aware of the spell cast by Mistress Wildes that lessened the power of your spell," she agreed. "And now we fear that between the demon and his legions, we are sorely outnumbered."

Sadness swept across the faces of all of the sisters, and they nodded slowly. "Yes, you are outnumbered," the first said. "But you are not outmatched, for there is power in you and through you that you have not tapped yet."

"What do you mean?" Finias asked. "How can we access that power?"

The second woman stepped forward and addressed Finias. "The hearts of the children will be turned to the parents, and the hearts of the parents will be turned to the children," she said.

"And that means?" Hazel asked.

The second woman smiled at Hazel, a wide smile, and nodded. "I am afraid that it is something you are going to have to discover on your own," she replied. "There is only so much we are able to share with you."

"No," Hazel replied, shaking her head. "No. Because this is not only about us now." She placed her hands on her belly. "This is about my baby. The safety of my child. So, you need to tell us more."

Sympathy filled the face of the second sister, and tears glistened in her eyes. "I too was carrying a child when we had to face the demon," she said softly. "When we agreed to this journey, I didn't realize I had made a choice for two, not one. I understand the fear and concern you are feeling."

Hazel's eyes filled with tears. "And your baby?" she asked hesitantly.

"She made the sacrifice with me," the second said sadly, and then she stepped back away from the portal opening.

"That doesn't mean that we have to follow in your path, does it?" Cat asked. "Blood was already spilled. A sacrifice was already made."

"Because of the changes that occurred, we cannot predict or guarantee that another sacrifice will not be called for," she replied. "But we will do whatsoever is in our power to help you in this fight."

"The legions," Henry said. "How do we fight the legions?"

67

"Divine power can defeat them," the third sister said.

"How do we tap into divine power?" Joseph asked.

"I can say no more at this time," the third sister replied and stepped away from the portal.

"This is crap," Donovan exclaimed. "You set us up one hundred years ago, and now you tell us you can't say any more. How are we supposed to fight this demon? How are we supposed to win?"

"Do not despair," the first sister said. "The way will be made known. The path will be clear."

"But…" Henry began.

The portal began to close before he could complete his sentence.

"The way will be made known," the first sister repeated. "The path will be made clear."

And then they were gone.

Chapter Eleven

"That was about as clear as mud," Hazel complained. "Why couldn't they just tell us how to destroy the demon?"

"Maybe they didn't know," Rowan replied. "Maybe they just hoped the way will be made clear."

Hazel shook her head. "If they don't know and we don't know, how are we supposed to win?"

"We're not supposed to despair," Henry said.

Hazel sent him a furious glance. "That's like saying calm down to a woman who's upset," she growled. "It only makes us angrier, and it does nothing to help the situation."

He chuckled softly and shook his head. "No, I'm not saying calm down," he explained. "But what I am saying is that our attitude approaching things makes a huge impact on how they are resolved."

"Come again?" Hazel asked.

"If you get up in the morning and say today is going to be a terrible day," he replied, 'it probably will be."

"Self-fulfilling prophecy," Cat inserted with a nod. She turned to Hazel. "Basically, peoples' beliefs influence their actions."

"So, if we don't despair and have confidence that we're going to beat it, it actually gives us an advantage," Hazel replied.

"Exactly," Henry said. "So, don't despair isn't just feel good talk, it's a warning that we all need to be positive about what's happening and how we are going to be able to overcome it."

Hazel took a deep breath. "Okay, we're going to win," she said slowly. "We're going to win. Now what?"

Dustin shifted on his pillow and slowly looked around the circle at the other members. "I think we need to think about what we were told," Dustin said. "Break things down for hidden meanings. Perhaps the sisters told us more than we realize."

"Okay, we are outnumbered but not outmatched," Rowan said. "And there is power within us that has not been tapped."

Henry nodded at Rowan. "Not just in us," Henry added. "But through us too."

"That's a little odd, isn't it?" Seamus asked, looking back at Henry. "Power through us, as if we were conduits to channel the energy into a certain direction."

"So, it's not our power?" Agnes asked. "But where would we get more power?"

"The hearts of the children will be turned to the parents, and the hearts of the parents will be turned to the children," Finias replied. "That's what she said."

There was silence for a long moment. "So, we have our parents here," Cat finally said, slowly speaking as she worked to figure it out in her own mind. "Does that mean we should be working with each other to improve our skills?"

"Aye, make sure that the knowledge we have is passed on to the next generation," Seamus inserted. "We should be training with each other."

"I think that's a good idea," Henry said. "But she said 'hearts,' not minds and not abilities."

"How do you turn the hearts of the children to their parents?" Joseph asked.

"Isn't that just natural?" Hazel asked. "Don't children automatically love their parents?"

Finias shook his head. "I know I've heard these words before," he said. "But delivered in a slightly different way."

"Oh, what an idjut I am," Seamus said. "And here I am a professor of religious studies. It's from Malachi in the Old Testament. *Behold, I will send you Elijah the prophet before the coming of the great and dreadful day of the Lord. And he will turn the hearts of the father to their children, and the hearts of the children to their fathers. Otherwise, I will come and strike the land with a curse.*"

Finias nodded. "Yes. Yes, that's it," he said.

"So, what does that mean?" Hazel asked.

"That's the question of the hour," Joseph said. "I mean, if we want to turn the children back to the parents, is that going back in time?"

Cat's eyes widened. "Maybe that's it," she said. "Remember when we were able to access Henry's memories and go back to when Patience dropped the book off at the Pratt Institute. Maybe there's more genetic inherited knowledge that we need to access."

Rowan nodded. "Sure, that makes sense," she agreed. "The sisters fought this demon, why wouldn't they have been faced with the legions too? What did they do to stop them?"

"That seems like a valid premise," Finias said. "But it seems that only Henry, because of Patience, and all of the Willoughby women would have any knowledge pertaining to the last curse. The rest of us aren't linked that way."

"But we should still try it, right?" Hazel asked.

Agnes nodded. "Yes. Yes, we should," she agreed. "Cat can help us access our memories, and Finias can help Cat access hers."

"Do we need to be within the circle," Hazel asked, putting her hand on her back and arching slightly. "I don't know how much longer I can sit on a pillow."

Joseph slid over behind Hazel and wrapped his arms around her waist. "Here, use me as a backrest," he said, kissing the top of her head.

She smiled up at him. "Okay, I'm totally comfortable now," she replied as she leaned back against him. "So, if we need to stay in the circle…"

"I don't think so," Agnes replied, smiling at Hazel and Joseph. "The house is protected, and if Cat finds something that should be only shared within the circle, she can save it until we are all together."

"So, should we disband the circle now?" Rowan asked.

"Not just yet," Seamus said. "Now, you might be perfectly on task with the talk of genetic knowledge. But

74

in case there's another message in there, I think we need to consider another explanation."

"And what would that be?" Henry asked.

"Striking the land with a curse," Seamus said. "And the great and dreadful day."

"What do you think that means, Seamus?" Agnes asked him.

He took a deep breath and lowered his head for a moment. Then he looked up and met her eyes. "Well, the great and dreadful day is the same day," he said slowly. "It's great for one side and dreadful for the other. Two sides of a coin. Whose side is going to end up on top, theirs or ours?"

Chapter Twelve

"Well, that was a cheery way to end the evening," Dustin muttered as he, Seamus, and Finias walked back to their cars parked in the Willoughby's driveway.

"I only said what I thought," Seamus said, defending himself. "And I thought we agreed that we shouldn't be hiding anything from each other."

Finias stopped walking and turned to the other two men. "We did agree to that. And in most cases, I believe that it serves its purpose. But I think I might have another interpretation of the message," he said, keeping his voice low. "And I don't want this shared with the others."

"What is it?" Seamus asked.

Finias shook his head. "An oath that you will not share or hint at what I'm about to tell you," he demanded, meeting their eyes.

"You have it," Seamus said. "My word."

Dustin nodded. "They don't need more worries placed upon them," he agreed. "I won't tell them anything unless I believe they would be in danger by not knowing it."

"I would never place any of them in danger," Finias exclaimed, his voice soft but firm.

"I believe you," Dustin replied. "Which is why I'm agreeing to the oath."

"Then follow me in your cars," Finias requested. "It would be better for me to show you as I explain my theory."

The three men separated into two cars—Finias in his vehicle and Dustin and Seamus in a rental car. Finias led the way down to the drive and turned away from town, heading down the country road toward the lake.

"Do you have any idea where he's taking us?" Seamus asked as they followed Finias down the dark and winding road.

"It's been quite a few years since I've been here," Dustin replied, slowing the car down as they went around a tight curve. "But I believe we're going toward the lake and the woods."

"Do you trust the man?" Seamus asked.

Dustin studied Seamus for a moment before turning his gaze back to the road. He considered Seamus' question for a few moments, and finally, he nodded his head. "Yes. I trust him," he said. "I believe he only has the best intentions for Agnes and the girls."

"I agree with your assessment," Seamus replied. "But I worry because we both know that visions that include yourself or your loved ones can often be skewed."

"That's true," Dustin agreed. "But at this point, I think we need to use any lead we can get. The entire premise of the spell has changed, and we are all walking blindly right now."

Seamus was quiet for a few moments, then spoke. "Perhaps not entirely blindly," he said quietly, then he turned to look at Dustin. "Did you have the dream then?"

Dustin nodded regretfully and kept his eyes on the road. "It's what led me here," he replied.

"Aye, me also," Seamus said. "Have you thought that the hearts of the children returning to their fathers could have anything to do with it?"

"I suppose that when children seek out their parents," Dustin said. "Especially older children, they often find them in a graveyard."

"It's a little like a Dickens' story, don't you think?" Seamus asked. "Here we are, as Ebenezer Scrooge, staring down at a vision of our own gravestones."

"And what did your gravestone say of you?" Dustin asked.

Seamus chuckled. "Are you hoping it said, 'They took on the demon and won?'" he asked.

Dustin laughed softly. "Well, that would be a nice epitaph, wouldn't it?"

"Aye," Seamus agreed. "But the truth is, I couldn't read the inscription. I couldn't even read the date."

Dustin sighed. "Me either," he said. "So, perhaps we live to be old men."

"A retirement party is not what sent me flying across the world to stand beside Agnes," Seamus replied.

"You're right," Dustin said. "And I've had a good life, so I won't be too sad to see it over."

"The hell with you," Seamus replied with a grin. "I'm planning on fighting every step of the way. I've pubs to visit and ladies to charm yet. However, if a sacrifice is needed to save my own, I'll gladly lay down my life."

"Magic has a price," Dustin said sadly.

"Aye, for all the wonder," Seamus agreed, "there is the reckoning."

Dustin slowed the car and turned into the park's entrance. "I've been here before," he said slowly.

"Aye, me too," Seamus said. "But it was in my dreams."

Chapter Thirteen

The blast from the plastic explosives was muffled by magic, and the doors on the prison cells sprung open. Ben Stoughton pushed his way through the doorway in front of the others and peered down the hall. "We have to be quick," he whispered harshly. "Any of you slow us down, and there will be hell to pay."

He moved forward, past the other cells in the area, followed by Wade, Neal, and Buck. The occupants of the other cells moved to the back of their cells quickly and quietly. They'd seen the cruelty and quick temper of Ben Stoughton and, even though it didn't make sense, they'd seen him use some kind of power to punish those who crossed him. They didn't want to be placed in his crosshairs.

When they reached the heavy steel door that closed off their wing, Ben paused and gave the mechanisms a cursory glance.

"We got lots more explosives," Wade offered, displaying the package Wanda had brought him. "We can blow this door to smithereens."

Ben turned and glowered at Wade, and Wade stumbled back. "You idiot," Ben snarled. "We blow this door, and every damn guard in the place will be here in minutes. Besides, the hinges are aluminum, we can take care of this ourselves."

He waved his hand at the door, and the hinge pins dropped to the ground. Ben reached up and pulled the door away from the frame, and they climbed through the opening.

"Which way?" Neal asked, his eyes wide with fright.

Ben turned to him. "You afraid, Abbott?" he sneered.

"I just...I just don't want to get shot," he whimpered.

"If I didn't know that you would betray me at the first chance you got, I would have left you behind in the cell," he replied. "Man up, or I will leave you here."

"But I thought you said you didn't trust him," Buck questioned.

Ben turned, glaring eyes on Buck. "If I leave him, he will be in no condition to tell anyone anything," he stated. "Now, follow me, we go to the left."

They hurried down a labyrinth of corridors and stairwells until they finally reached a door that was marked for laundry. Ben opened the door slowly. They could hear the whoosh and whir of the giant machines cleaning the laundry for the prison. Ben scanned the area and could see none of the workers down there. "It's clear," he whispered. "Follow me."

They worked their way across the cement floor, past giant washing machines and dryers, water heaters and pipes, until they reached a door at the back of the building. Ben turned to Wade. "Did you take care of this alarm?" he asked.

Wade bobbed his head in response. "Yeah, yeah. I took care of them all," he replied.

Ben pushed on the metal bar to open the door, and suddenly the light above the door began to blink bright red. "Damn it," Ben growled, glaring at Wade. "We gotta run for it."

They dashed out of the door and ran across the loading dock, jumping off onto the driveway. "What now?" Buck asked, his voice shaking.

"We're not inside an iron building anymore," Ben replied irritably. "Hide yourselves."

Suddenly all four men disappeared from view.

Buck laughed. "This is great, no one can see us," he crowed.

"Idiot," Ben replied, his voice low. "They can still hear you."

Wanda's car pulled up at the end of the drive. She quickly got out and opened the doors closest to the prison. She could sense the presence of the men, but couldn't see how close they were to her car.

"Um, Miss, are you okay?"

Wanda turned to see the young officer from earlier walking towards her. He was dressed in his civilian clothes, so he must have been off duty.

She smiled at him. "I'm fine," she said. "But I left some lunch in my car, and it smells so badly that I had to stop and air things out."

He chuckled softly. "I've done the same thing myself," he replied. "It was cheese. I think the smell lasted for weeks."

He glanced around and then shrugged "Well, you might want to move your car a little further down the road," he suggested. "The guards don't like people or cars loitering near the prison."

"Oh, of course," she replied. "That makes sense."

She turned to see that the car was sitting lower to the ground, so the men must have gotten in. She turned back to the young officer. "I'll just…"

She gasped as she watched the young man tear at his throat, trying to breath. His face was turning blue, and

85

his eyes were bulging. She turned to the car. "Stop it," she yelled. "He didn't see you. He didn't see anything."

She heard the body hit the ground and turned as guilt and horror washed over her. She didn't need to feel for a pulse, she knew the young guard was dead.

"Get in the car, Wanda," Ben ordered. "Or you can join him."

She stumbled around the car, tears blinding her, and slipped into the driver's seat. "Why?" she wheezed. "Why did you have to kill him."

Ben, appearing next to her, shrugged easily. "He was in my way," he replied. "Now go."

Chapter Fourteen

"Well, that's interesting," Cat exclaimed, she was sitting facing Henry on the couch, her hands on either side of Henry's head. Henry's eyes were closed, and he was breathing deeply as if he were asleep.

"What?" Rowan asked softly, leaning forward in her chair across from the couch.

Cat opened her eyes for a moment and turned to her sister. "Give me a minute," she requested. "I want to be sure we capture all the details."

She closed her eyes again and turned back to Henry. "Okay, Henry," she whispered. "Let's go back to the night of the spell again."

Cat was suddenly standing next to Henry inside a dark cave.

"Are you sure we should do this?" Henry asked her, glancing at the darkness looming before them.

"If we want to find out what we're going to be facing, we need to find out what happened the night of the spell," she replied. "But are you okay with doing this?"

He took a deep breath and nodded. "Welcome to my memories," he said, holding his hand forward as a sign they should both proceed.

"So, are we here, or is this like *A Christmas Carol*, and what we are going to see are just shadows of the past?" he asked as they slowly walked down the dirt path.

"Well, we're accessing this place through your memories," she replied thoughtfully. "But, I'm not sure if these are shadows, or our spirits have been transported."

"An out of body experience to the past," Henry mused. "Well, that an interesting hypothesis."

The path was not straight, and as it angled downward, the height of the ceiling lessened. Soon, Henry was walking with his head bowed to avoid the sharp stone. They turned another corner, and an outcropping caught him on the side of his temple.

"Ouch," he said, stopping and rubbing his head. He pulled his hand away and noticed the blood. "I believe that if we can bleed, we can also…"

He closed his mouth and shook his head. "Never mind," he said abruptly and started to walk.

Cat caught his arm and stopped him. He turned back to her with a questioning look in his eye.

"If we can bleed, we can die," she stated.

He inhaled deeply and nodded. "Yes," he agreed. "That about sums it up."

"Well, then we better be sure we get out of here before something happens," she replied.

They continued going downhill for another half-mile and then stopped as the path stopped at the opening of a large chamber. Several sizeable boulders edged the round cavern chamber, and Cat and Henry hid behind them to observe the witches in the room before them.

"Look," Henry whispered. "There's the Willoughby quaternary knot." He pointed to a circle identical to the one in the Willoughby great room that had been somehow carved into the stone floor.

"It's just like the one at home," she said. "I always thought they just needed three."

"Maybe Patience was there for more than just record-keeping," Henry mused.

Four women stood on one of each of the four circles that combined to make the knot.

They were dressed in long robes of white with garlands of bright maple leaves in their hair, their hair loose and flowing down their backs. Each carried a wand that was carved from a Rowan branch with a glowing crystal at the end. They chanted softly as they built their protective circle, walking around the knot, and sealing it from outside threats.

"It's very similar to what you do," Henry whispered.

Cat nodded. "But if they are sealed off, how do they plan to capture the demon?" she wondered.

Suddenly, the stone in the center of the circle, the place where all four parts of the knot entwined, began to crack, and a red glow filled in the gap. The witches pointed their wands toward the center and began to chant softly.

Then Patience stepped a little closer to the center and raised her voice:

> *We come this night, this Samhain eve*
>
> *To sacrifice for another's deed*
>
> *That done in ignorance and blithe,*
>
> *Has released a demon on this night*

The center of the circle cracked further, and the cave shook. Henry and Cat grabbed hold of the boulder to keep from falling. Then Patience stepped back, and the first Willoughby sister stepped forward and spoke.

> *We three the sacrifice will be.*
>
> *The fourth will save our legacy.*
>
> *The power within us holds you at bay,*
>
> *Until we fight another day.*

Red, molten lava bubbled in the center of the circle, and the large disk of stone wobbled, then sunk beneath the surface of the boiling rock. The next Willoughby sister stepped forward, this time standing beside the sister that just spoke. The first sister placed her hand on her sister's shoulder and remained at her side. The second sister spoke:

Three times forty we proclaim,

The binding spell to stop your reign,

And when the years have been consumed,

Three from one will seal your doom.

The cave rocked, and dust and gravel fell down from the ceiling. The lava bubbled with more intensity, melting off more of the center of the knot. The two sisters near the center and the last sister stepped forward between the other two. Sisters on either end placed their hands on the shoulders of the last sister. But before she spoke, she turned to Patience.

"You must step out of the circle now," she said. "Go to the edge of the room and record the spell, then you must run out of here."

"Why?" Patience asked. "Why must I leave?"

"Because he has more strength than we thought," the sister replied, shaking her head. "Something has happened. Something has changed. But we cannot go back now. We need you, dear Patience, to save the spell and to protect our legacy."

"But..." Patience began to argue.

"Now," the sister exclaimed, and then she stepped forward and looked down into the bubbling pit. Patience stumbled back, standing just in front of the boulders that Cat and Henry were hiding behind.

We cast this binding spell on thee,

And sacrifice our lives to pay the fee.

With the power of the Willoughbys

We seal your fate, as mote it be.

The sisters all pointed their wands into the center of the circle as a surge of white energy surged around the circle, then through their bodies and into their wands. The energy, like bolts of lightning, cascaded forward into the lava. The cave trembled, and the hole in the center of the circle enlarged with lava spewing up into the air. The sisters stepped back, to stay on solid ground, but they never once wavered, their wands fixed on the center of the knot.

Patience stepped further back, her eyes wide as she watched the fight between good and evil.

The crevice grew bigger, large chunks of the carved rock falling into the molten liquid. The sisters stepped back again, as the heat from the center scorched them.

"Now, Patience," called the last sister. "You must leave now."

Patience ran past Henry and Cat, and down the path that led out of the cave.

"Could she see us?" Henry asked.

Cat shook her head. "I don't know," she replied. "But maybe we ought to…"

The words dried in her throat as she watched the molten liquid divide into three streams and gush towards each of the sisters. For a moment, the burning, red liquid was held at bay by the lightening energy expelled from the wands, but slowly, Cat could see that the energy was being consumed. The lava was getting closer and closer to them.

"Sisters," said the one in the middle. "It is time."

The two on each end stepped closer to the one in the middle and placed their wands in their outer hands. Then they wrapped their free arms around the middle sister, uniting all three, combining their power and the power of their wands. Then, in one voice, they repeated the last lines of the spell:

We cast this binding spell on thee,

And sacrifice our lives to pay the fee.

With the power of the Willoughbys

We seal your fate, as mote it be.

"Henry!" Patience's voice rang in Henry's head. "You must leave now!"

Henry grabbed Cat's arm. "We have to go, now!" he cried.

As they turned to go, he saw the black mist unfurl in the middle of the knot and move past the sisters toward them. He grabbed Cat's hand and ran. He could feel the malevolence following them as they rushed back towards the cave opening.

Rowan watched as Henry's body moved in response to an unseen threat, his face flinching and his arms jerking.

"It's okay, Henry," Cat tried to assure him as they ran down the dirt path. "We're both safe. Take a deep breath."

Henry shook his head. "It's not safe in there," he said, his voice slurred, as he felt the evil catching up to them. "Cat, we need to get out."

"What?" Cat asked, confused. "What's not…" And then she felt it too.

Cat's gasp of fear had Rowan jumping to her feet and dashing across the room. "What?" she demanded.

Ignoring her sister, Cat opened her eyes and took a deep breath. "Henry, when I count to three, you will be awake and alert," she said quickly. "And no longer in this hypnotic state. One, two, three!"

Henry's eyes flashed open, and Cat immediately pulled her hands away, breaking the connection.

Henry fell back against the couch, gasping for air.

"How did he do that?" Cat stammered. "How could he enter your memories?"

"Maybe he didn't enter," Henry breathed. "Maybe he was part of the memory itself. All I know is that we just made it out of there with no time to spare."

"What just happened?!?" Rowan demanded.

"We saw the sisters cast the spell," Cat said.

"Patience was part of the circle," Henry added. "She was there until the sacrifice had to be made. Then they forced her to break the circle and run."

"And somehow, when we accessed the memory, the demon accessed it too," Cat said, her voice shaking.

"It was like when he was chasing us in the ether. He was there. He was so close."

Henry reached over and put his hand on Cat's arm to comfort her. "But he wasn't close enough," he said, meeting her eyes. "We escaped. We're fine. And we have more information now than we did before. Important information."

"What information?" Rowan asked.

Cat stood up and motioned for Rowan to take her place. "You sit with Henry while I get the others," she said. "I think everyone needs to hear this."

Rowan slipped down onto the couch and wrapped her arms around Henry. "You scared me," she whispered, laying her head against his chest.

"I scared me," he admitted, kissing the top of her head. "One moment, we're watching the spell being cast, and then I see some kind of black cloud forming and coming at us."

She nodded. "That's how it was with us," she said. "And terrifying doesn't begin to describe it."

"I agree," he said. "Luckily, as soon as I pointed it out to Cat, she got us out of there."

Rowan leaned back and met Henry's eyes. "What do you think would have happened if he had caught you?" she asked. "I mean, you were in Patience's memories. You weren't even there."

Henry nodded slowly. "That's a very good question," he replied. "Was he really there, or was that a memory? All I know is that it felt real, and I wanted to get away as soon as we could."

Then he reached up and touched his forehead. It was still tender from the hit in the cave. How does a memory leave a mark, he wondered?

She leaned forward again, snuggling against his chest. "Well, I'm glad you got out of there," she said. "And I'm so grateful you saw him before he could hurt you or Cat."

He kissed the top of her head again and smiled. "Well, actually, I think I might have had a bit of help," he said. "I heard Patience call out to me."

A tear slipped from Rowan's eye and trailed down her cheek. "I'm so glad she can still reach you," she whispered hoarsely.

He hugged her tightly. "And when she's able, I'm sure she'll reach out to you too," he replied.

"I hope so," Rowan said softly. "I really hope so."

Chapter Fifteen

"Should we invite Finias, Dustin, and Seamus?" Agnes asked as they gathered in the living room. "I can call them."

Cat shook her head. "I can fill them in tomorrow," she answered. "I'd really like to talk about this while it's fresh in our minds."

Henry nodded. "I agree," he said. "It isn't so urgent that they need to hear it tonight, but we certainly need to record it tonight to get down all of the facts."

Agnes sat down on a chair nearest to the fireplace and looked around the room at her daughters and their partners. "Should we form a circle?" Agnes asked.

Cat glanced over at Henry, and he shook his head. "No, we had a little trouble with the demon earlier, but I think it was just because of the circumstances," he said. "I think we should be able to talk about this within the safety of the house."

"What kind of trouble did you have with the demon?" Donovan asked.

"He was somehow able to enter the memories we were accessing and seemed to be trying to attack or stop us," Cat explained.

"How the hell does he get into your memories?" Joseph asked.

Henry shrugged. "Well, first, they were Patience's memories that somehow she downloaded into my brain. Cat calls it…"

"Genetic inherited knowledge," Cat inserted. "But I think in this case it's a little more than that. I believe Patience, as Henry put it, downloaded the information Henry would need – we all would need – to complete the spell."

"But you still didn't answer my question," Joseph said. "How did the demon get into Patience's memories?"

"It could be that he was already there," Henry replied. "Because the memory included him. Or maybe it wasn't a memory, but more of an out-of-body trip to the past. I don't have much more of an explanation than that."

"Okay, why don't we let them take it from the top," Rowan suggested.

"Good idea," Donovan concurred.

Cat clasped her hands together and nodded. "As you know, we decided that we ought to try to access any memories or knowledge that might help us," she explained. "And I thought I'd start with Henry because he already had some information from the past that helped us find the grimoire."

"That makes sense," Donovan said.

"So, I hypnotized Henry in order to free his thoughts from any encumbrance and make my job a little easier," she explained. "Then I went back to the area in his mind that we'd accessed earlier."

Henry nodded. "I could see Patience walking down the street again towards the Pratt Institute," he added, and then he paused and looked over at Cat. "And then I had the weirdest sensation that I was going backwards."

Cat chuckled and nodded. "Well, I wanted to see what happened earlier," she said. "So, I accessed Patience when I first found her and then tried to move backward on the timeline."

"That was brilliant," he said. "So, we went back, and I could see that morning when she finished writing everything in the grimoire, as well as the early morning hours when she finally got back to her home."

"Then we could see the ceremony," Cat inserted. "It was in the woods, but it wasn't on the granite stone with the crack."

"Where was it?" Hazel asked.

Henry shook his head. "I'm not sure," he said. "But I feel like we were in a cave." He turned to Cat. "Is that what you felt?"

She nodded. "Yes, I knew it was enclosed, but you're right, it probably was a cave," she agreed. "But carved into the floor…"

"Into the stone floor," Henry added.

"Right," Cat agreed. "Was a duplicate of the circle we have in the house."

"Exactly," Henry confirmed. "The same quaternary knot, the same Celtic symbols, but instead of wood, it was carved into stone."

"How many places did it hold?" Agnes asked.

"The same as ours," Cat replied to her mother. "There were places for four."

"We watched them form the circle, and then place the spell," Henry said.

Then Henry and Cat glanced at each other for a moment. "We also saw them just before they died," Cat finally said. "They told Patience to run away, but she paused at what must have been the mouth of the cave and looked back."

"Did the demon kill them?" Agnes asked.

Henry shook his head. "I don't think so," he said. "Because then he wouldn't have been confined. I think the amount of energy needed to contain him was too much for their bodies to handle. It pulled everything out of them."

"If Patience had stayed?" Rowan asked.

"I don't think her presence in the circle would have made a difference," Cat replied. "The power was far above their ability to absorb and control it. That's why they sent Patience away, and she made it out of the cave just before it collapsed."

"They were buried in a cave-in?" Hazel gasped.

"Yes," Henry said. "The power that sealed the demon in also sealed the cave. But, from what we see through Patience's eyes, they were already near death – if not already dead when it happened."

"So, their final resting place is under the rock near the lake," Agnes said sadly.

"Well, the final resting place of their bodies," Henry replied. "We know that their spirits weren't trapped in there because they've been guiding your family for generations."

Agnes smiled at him and nodded. "Thank you for that reminder," she said. "It's better to remember that their sacrifice didn't trap them, only the demon."

"Yeah," Hazel added. "I would hate to think they were trapped under those rocks for all these years."

Chapter Sixteen

"All I see is a large pile of rocks," Seamus said as he stood next to Finias and Dustin on a ledge one hundred feet below the granite rock.

"I dreamt of this place," Finias said. "But there were no rocks, it was open."

"How far back did it go?" Dustin asked.

Finias closed his eyes to bring back the image he saw in his vision. "About half a mile back," he said. "It had a narrow opening at the start of the cave, but then at about ten feet, it opened up."

Dustin nodded, then looked around, his hands resting easily on his hips, and saw a large open field about seventy-five feet away. "Well, that looks like a good spot," he muttered.

"A good spot for what?" Finias asked.

"This," Dustin replied, pointing at the rocks and then swiping his arms in the direction of the field.

Suddenly, the rocks disappeared from the cave and reappeared in a large pile in the middle of the field.

Finias smiled. "And now we know where Hazel gets her ability," he said.

"It comes in handy when you're in engineering," Dustin replied, then he slowly walked closer to the cave. "I can't vouch for the stability of the overhang, though. What we need here is a little more light."

He closed his eyes for a moment, then opened them and looked inside the cave.

"The way before us is dark and closed,

And it's secrets we cannot see,

Through light its secrets will be exposed,

As we ask, so mote it be."

Suddenly the cave was filled with light, and Dustin stepped up closer to the entrance. "That corner there," he said, pointing to the back corner, "looks like it could use some extra support."

He closed his eyes, then opened them and waved his arms, and a steel beam and support now stood in that

109

corner. He turned to Finias and Seamus. "Remind me to send a check to the local construction yard in the morning," he said easily, then he walked further into the cave.

"Amazing," Seamus said, following Dustin into the cave.

Dustin stopped and looked back. "Aren't you concerned for your safety?" he asked.

Seamus grinned. "No, I'm a healer," he replied. "I thought I'd best stay close to you in case you drop part of the ceiling on your head."

Dustin laughed. "Well, good point," he agreed. "Do stay close then."

They examined the cave's structure with Dustin adding a few more supports, and then, once they felt it was stable, they started to look at the rest of the cave. The floor of the cave was covered with a thin layer of dirt and plant residue from the removed rocks.

"It feels like there is some residual energy coming from the center of the cave, over here," Finias said, walking away from the other two men towards the energy. He was almost to the center when Seamus darted forward, grabbed his arm, and pulled him back.

"What?" Finias exclaimed.

"Look out, man," Seamus said, pointing to the ground in front of Finias where he would have stepped next. "There's nothing under the thin layer of dirt there."

Finias reached out his foot and tapped lightly on the surface. A large piece of crusted over dirt cracked apart and plunged down, leaving a huge gaping hole in the ground.

"It was like it was superheated dirt that formed a hard crust," Dustin said, looking down at it.

Finias then looked up and could see a narrow fissure that extended from the cave roof up through the rock to the surface one hundred feet above them. "This is probably how the demon accessed the rock face," Finias said slowly. "He came up from the hole below, up through the rocks, and moved the molten rock with him."

"Which would explain the dirt crust," Dustin agreed.

Seamus stepped back and pushed the dirt beyond the hole around with his feet. "Dustin, my good fellow," he said. "Can you sweep away this layer of dirt with one of those arm swings you do?"

"Sure. Why?" Dustin asked.

"I believe there's something carved into the cave floor," Seamus replied.

With a quick wave of his hand, Dustin moved the dirt away from the hole and moved it to the corners of the cave. There, where the dirt had been, was a clear drawing of a Celtic circle.

"This is where your energy came from," Seamus said to Finias. "It's the Willoughby quaternary knot."

"This is where they cast their spell," Dustin agreed.

"And this is what I saw in my vision," Finias added.

Dustin turned to Finias and folded his arms across his chest. "And now it's time for you to tell us about the rest of your vision," he stated firmly.

"You know that visions that include yourself or family members are often not correct," Finias replied.

Dustin nodded. "Yes, but I'll take my chances that your closer to right than wrong," he said. "Besides, at least it will give us an idea of what we're dealing with."

Finias nodded slowly and walked to the edge of the knot. "I saw us, the three of us here," he said slowly, not only remembering, but reliving the vision "And another, Agnes, is here too."

"One for each of the circles," Seamus said. "That makes sense."

"The center of the circle was broken away, as it is now," Finias continued. "But it was filled with a pillar of molten rock."

Dustin looked up above the circle and could see stars through a hole in the top of the cavern. "It sounds like this is the first floor, and the granite rock on the top of the hill is the penthouse," he said. "It would take a hell of a lot of pressure to push magma up that high."

"Not magma," Seamus corrected him. "Brimstone. And it only takes magic, albeit the wrong kind of magic."

"We cast a circle," Finias said. "To protect our children from the legions."

"So, we come down here to make sure they are only fighting the demon," Seamus said with a nod. "As it was first written. Take them out at the pass, so to speak."

Finias inhaled deeply. "That was our intent," he said softly.

"So, it didn't end well," Dustin inserted.

"There was an explosion," he replied. "Magma shot out in all directions. I didn't see our deaths, but…"

"But although witches, we are still mortal," Dustin said.

"Did it make a difference?" Seamus asked. "Did we stop the legions?"

Finias shook his head. "I don't know," he answered sincerely. "I can't say."

"Well, if the brimstone is heading horizontally instead of vertically," Seamus said, his mouth set with determination. "Then I'd say we at least gave them an advantage."

"A slight reprieve," Dustin agreed.

"And the loss of their mother?" Finias asked. "How will they deal with that?"

Seamus sighed sadly. "Ah, well, at least they will have the ability to grieve for her," he remarked softly "They will have their lives to live and remember."

"How will Agnes feel about this?" Dustin asked.

"I think she already knows," Finias informed them. "I think she's seen the vision too."

Chapter Seventeen

Agnes, dressed in a flowing nightgown in deep plum, walked across her dark bedroom and reached over the window seats to open the windows and let in the cool, autumn air. The night was clear, and she could see a scattering of stars in the sky. In the distance, she could hear the distinct cry of an owl, crying for his mate through the treetops. And closer still, the yaps of a pack of coyotes echoed through the night.

She slipped onto a window seat, laid her back against the wall, and wrapped her arms around her knees. She loved to rest here, in this space that was on the brink of both worlds – home and nature. She leaned to the side, resting her cheek against the cool pane of glass, looking up through the treetops to the constellations and listening to the soothing sounds of nature that had always welcomed her.

She sighed. Less than a week. Less than a week and life as she had always known it would be changed.

Less than a week, and she would either be triumphant or…

She closed her eyes and shook her head.

"No," she said softly. "I do not want to think about that."

A soft whine from the foot of her bed interrupted her thoughts, she turned and smiled at the wolf who had lifted his head and was staring at her.

"What? Am I getting too morose for you?" she asked with a sad smile.

He laid down his giant head with a dramatic canine sigh of his own.

She laughed softly. "Oh, I see, I'm not the only one who can sigh about my problems," she said, slipping off the window seat and walking over to him. She sat next to him on the bed and wrapped her arms around him, burying her face in his furry neck. "If, for some reason, I'm not around, you will look after them, won't you?" she whispered.

Fuzzy growled softly and shook his head.

117

Agnes sat up, offended. "You don't know that," she insisted. "Of course, I might be fine. But, you know, things could happen."

The wolf stared into her eyes with calm assurance.

"Don't," Agnes chastised the beast. "Don't tell me to calm down. You do realize, don't you, that telling someone to calm down has the opposite effect on them?"

Fuzzy yawned widely and then put his head on his paws.

"I am not being dramatic," she replied. "Things could happen. Bad things could happen. We don't know…"

Fuzzy lifted his paw and placed it on her arm. She stopped talking and nodded. "You're right," she admitted with chagrin. "We don't know, do we?" She rubbed the wolf on the top of his head. "So, what do you suggest, oh wise wolf?"

He whined softly, dug his head deeper into the blankets, and then closed his eyes.

She laughed and nodded. "A good night's sleep, and things will look better in the morning," she said. "Good advice, dear friend." She leaned down and kissed him on the top of his head. "Sweet dreams."

Climbing to the top of the bed, she slipped underneath her comforter, adjusted her pillow, and let the worries of the day fade away. In a few minutes, she was sleeping soundly, and her mind was carried away to an earlier time in her life.

"I'm home," Agnes called as she pushed open the kitchen door and tossed her books on the counter. "And I'm starving!"

"There are fresh vegetables in the fridge," her mother called from the laundry room.

"Fresh vegetables?" she whispered with a grimace. *"I'm not a rabbit."*

"There are also chocolate chip cookies in the cookie jar," her mother added. *"In case you're not a rabbit."*

Laughing, Agnes lifted the top off the chubby witch cookie jar and snatched two cookies, then made her way to the laundry room. "I know you didn't hear me," she said to her mom. She leaned against the door jamb and, as she chewed on a cookie, studied her mom bent over and pulling sheets from the dryer.

Her mom looked over and grinned. "Hear you say what dear?" she asked innocently.

Agnes pushed herself off the door jamb and walked over to the dryer. "How did you hear me grumble about not being a rabbit?" she asked.

Her mother's smile widened. "Magic," she teased.

"Mom," Agnes sighed in response. "That's so lame."

Her mother shook her head. "No, not lame, magic," she replied, pulling the final sheets out of the dryer and closing it. "And that will be one of the lessons I teach you tonight."

Agnes' face dropped. "Oh," she said softly.

120

"What?" her mother asked.

"About tonight," Agnes began, then shook her head. "Never mind. Tonight's good. Tonight's cool."

"What about tonight?" her mother asked again.

Agnes shrugged. "No big deal," she said. "Just a football game."

"And you were invited to go?" her mother asked.

Shrugging again, the teenaged Agnes played it off. "Really, Mom, games can be so lame," she said. "And cold. It will probably be cold."

Her mother turned and placed her hands on Agnes' shoulders. "You need to have joy in this life," she said, meeting her daughter's eyes. "If there is one thing I want to impress on you, even with your responsibilities and challenges, you need to find joy. You need to take time for fun, friends, and family. You need to make memories. It's important."

"More important than magic?" Agnes asked. "More important than our duty?"

"The most important," she replied. "What good is magic, or anything else, without happiness and joy? You should go to that football game. You should cheer for your team, eat food that's terrible for you, and have fun."

Agnes met her mother's eyes. "Really?" she asked. "What about my lesson?"

"I just taught you the most important lesson of life," she said, her eyes somber and truthful. "If you can remember this when hard times come and when life presents its challenges, I have done my job. Find joy, my dear sweet Agnes, always find joy."

Agnes sat up in her bed and looked around the darkened room. Fuzzy was snoring softly at the foot of the bed, his feet twitching as he chased something in his dreams.

"Find joy," she said softly, remembering the dream. "And how, my dear sweet mother, do I find joy in the midst of all of this turmoil?"

"Well, you have three beautiful daughters who have all found exceptional matches."

Gasping, Agnes turned toward the sound.

The translucent shape of her mother stood in front of the windows near the window seat Agnes had occupied just a few hours ago.

"Mom," she whispered, her voice trembling. "Is that really you?"

"Of course, it's me," her mother replied gently. "I'm always nearby, watching over you."

"But…but, I've never seen you before," Agnes said.

Her mother shrugged easily. "There are rules," she said. "But occasionally there are exceptions. And when the dream didn't work, I decided that I needed to come and talk to you in person…well, in spirit." She laughed softly.

"You sent me the dream?" Agnes asked.

Her mother nodded. "And the memories," she replied. "To try and guide you to the right path."

"What is the right path?"

Her mother sighed impatiently. "Agnes, what happens in the next few days?" she asked.

"Samhain, of course, the night we need to face the demon," Agnes replied.

"Can you change that?"

Agnes shook her head. "No. No, I can't change that," she said, then a sudden thought came to her mind. Maybe her mother was suggested they could change their destiny. "Can I?"

"No, darling, you can't," her mother replied. "I'm sorry. I wish I could say you could, but that's not your path."

Agnes nodded. "Okay, so if I can't change what happens, what's the point?" she asked.

"You can't change what happens, but you can change how you deal with it," her mother replied. "You can worry and fret. You can be discouraged and morose. Or, you can decide to live the next few days celebrating the family you have, the love you share, and the blessings you have been given."

124

"I used to hate these kinds of talks," Agnes muttered.

Her mother laughed with delight. "Yes, you did," she replied. "But only because I was always right."

"Yes, you were," she admitted, her heart feeling less burdened. "I can't change what happens, but I can enjoy the time we have left."

"Or the time before a new beginning for your family," her mother suggested. "We don't know what will happen, but I have always had faith that good eventually overcomes evil."

"So, what should I do?" Agnes asked. "How do I find joy in the midst of all of this?"

"Instead of a day of dread, turn Samhain into a day of celebration," she suggested.

Agnes shook her head. "I don't understand," she replied.

"Celebrate the love you have all found during this journey," she said. "Have a handfasting."

"What? In the middle of all this, I'm supposed to plan three weddings?" Agnes asked, astonished.

Her mother laughed. "Well, it will certainly keep your mind off other things, won't it?" she replied. Then her smile fell, and she met her daughter's eyes. "Seal your daughters to their partners so they can enjoy the eternities together, no matter what happens later that evening. Fill yourselves so full of joy and love that no power can defeat you."

"You're right," she whispered. "I know in my heart that you're right."

Her mother smiled at her and then started to fade away. "Sweet dreams, Agnes," she whispered. "Get all the rest you can, because you're going to need it."

"I love you, Mom," Agnes said as her mother's form faded into the night.

"I love you too, darling," the soft replied echoed around the room.

Settling back down onto her pillows, Agnes smiled, her daughters were all getting married in less than

126

a week. She wondered what they were going to say about

it.

Chapter Eighteen

"No," Cat exclaimed, slapping her wallet on the kitchen counter. "No. Just no."

Agnes sat at the table, her hands wrapped around a steaming mug of chamomile tea and a serene expression on her face. "Okay," she replied easily.

"Wait, why not?" Hazel asked, as she bit into a banana nut muffin and slipped onto a stool next to the counter.

"Well, because it's too soon," Rowan supplied as she added water to her water bottle. "I mean, it's less than a week away. Weddings, even handfastings, take longer to put together than that."

"So?" Hazel asked. "I built the apartment over the barn in thirty minutes. Some people would say that normally it takes longer to do that too, but we've got a special set of skills."

"Well, that's not the point," Cat said. "I don't know about the rest of you, but how can you even think about something like this when…"

"We don't know if we'll be alive by then?" Hazel asked, her eyes wide with sadness.

"I didn't mean…" Cat began.

"Don't you remember, we're not supposed to despair," Hazel said. "We are supposed to be hopeful, and what's more hopeful than a handfasting?"

Rowan sighed. "She does have a point," she said to Cat. "And it would be lovely to be sealed as one before we have to face the demon."

"And his legions," Cat added and then turned to Hazel. "I'm sorry. I'm sorry. Maybe you're right. Maybe we all need something like this—something joyful, to bring up our spirits."

Agnes sipped her tea again, enjoying the debate and relishing in the fact that she hadn't had to say a word.

Cat turned to look at her mother. "You're awfully quiet over there," she said.

Agnes smiled and shrugged. "Really, it's up to you three," she said. "I'm all for it, as you know, but it will be the three of you, not me."

"No," Rowan said as an idea came to mind. "No, it needs to be four. Everything, the quaternary knot on the floor, the spell that was cast in the cavern, even three from one–the sum is four. We need to make this a celebration of four."

Agnes' brow wrinkled, and she shook her head. "How are you going to find another couple?" she asked.

"We already have one," Rowan replied. "You momma. You will renew your vows."

Agnes' serene smile vanished, and she shook her head. "No, that's not going to work," she replied. "I mean, Finias has not even… No, it should be the three of you."

"Rowan's right," Cat said. "We all can see that you and Finias never stopped loving each other. It makes perfect sense."

"No, it doesn't," Agnes said, setting her tea down, pushing back her chair and standing. Things were getting

130

totally out of control, and she needed to set them all straight. "Now, girls, you need to listen to me."

Hazel grinned. "Why Mom?" she asked. "We never have before?"

Agnes glared at her daughter.

"Catalpa, Rowan, and Hazel," Agnes exclaimed.

"See, you're not that old, you still remember our names," Hazel quipped.

A smile trembled on Agnes' lips, but she bit it back. She knew that a smile would just show weakness.

Hazel leaned forward on the counter. "I saw the smile," she whispered. "Admit it, we won."

Agnes shook her head. "You did not win," she said. "This is not a contest."

"No," Cat said, walking over and putting her arms around her mother's shoulders. "This is a celebration of love. And it's a celebration of the full circle we've traveled to put us here, where we are right now. You and Finias have to be a part of it to make it complete."

Agnes sighed softly. "He hasn't asked me," she admitted.

"Don't worry about that," Hazel inserted. "I can take care of that."

"No!" Agnes, Cat, and Rowan exclaimed at the same time.

Hazel laughed and nodded. "See, now there's something you can all agree on."

Agnes clapped her hand over her mouth and shook her head. "No, Hazel," she said with contrition. "I didn't mean it. I mean, I did, but I didn't."

Hazel got up, walked over to her mom, and copied Cat's actions, also putting her arms around her shoulders. "I love you," she said earnestly. "And I want you to be as happy as I am. I think Finias is awesome and I can tell he is totally in love with you. The right moment will happen. It's meant to be." Then she looked at her sisters. "And I'm in charge of the food."

She leaned forward, kissed her mom's cheek, and then stepped back. "Okay, I'm driving into town to get

132

supplies for the goats and to pick up a few things I'm craving. Text me anything else you'd like."

Once the door closed. Rowan turned to Cat in alarm. "She's in charge of the food?" she moaned. "Everything is going to be fried."

Chapter Nineteen

Walking into the feed store was not as simple as Hazel wanted it to be. Only a few months earlier, Harley, the owner of the store and a man she'd known all her life, had kidnapped her for the coven. The Willoughbys had not pressed charges against him, or even sought revenge in their own way. But instead, they had just continued with their own personal fight against the demon and those who supported him.

Hazel walked up the aisle that held supplements for all kinds of farm animals, realizing the joy she used to experience when she entered the store was now gone. She stopped halfway up the aisle, nearly turning around and going back to her truck, but her goats needed feed and other supplies, and she didn't feel like driving an hour away to the next closest store.

"Hazel?" Harley's tentative and surprised voice came from behind her.

She slowly turned and met the eyes of the man who had betrayed her trust. But he couldn't meet hers, he immediately lowered his face and shook his head. "I can't tell you how ashamed I am," he stammered. "Can't tell you how bad I feel."

"Why did you do it?" Hazel asked before she could stop herself.

He glanced up at her, his eyes red-rimmed and weary. "I didn't know," he whispered. "It's like it wasn't me. Like things were coming from my own mouth that I didn't even recognize." Then he shook his head and took a deep breath. "But, I ain't blaming it all on the Master getting hold of my mind. 'Cause some of the things I did, some of the things I said, it was me. So, I just don't know – I got twisted up in my head."

He pulled an old handkerchief out of his pocket and blotted his face. "Never thought I was someone who would choose money or security over a friend," he said sadly, shaking his head. "Never thought I was so weak."

Hazel exhaled slowly and looked at the sad man in front of her. He was right, he was weak, and the demon had played on his insecurities and his weaknesses in order to use him. He wasn't totally blameless, but she found her heart wasn't filled with the anger that used to be there.

"Harley," she finally said. "I don't know how I feel right now. I can tell you that I'm sad because I thought we were friends. I don't know if I can ever trust you again. But I don't hate you, and I don't wish anything bad to happen to you. I really hope that you can turn away from the coven and that demon. I hope it, not for me, but for your own sake."

He nodded slowly, and this time the handkerchief was used for his eyes. "Thank you, Hazel," he said. "That's far more than I deserve."

She shook her head. "No, Harley," she said. "We all deserve a second chance."

"Thank you," he repeated, and he inhaled deeply. "So, how can I help you?"

Smiling, she reached into her purse and pulled out a list. "I need supplies for my goats," she said.

He took the list, scanned it quickly, and nodded. "Tell you what," he said. "I'll pull this list together and have it out to your place by early afternoon. Does that work?"

"I have my truck," she said.

He shook his head and glanced at her belly. "I'll send one of my guys to your place with instructions that he's to carry the feed bags into the barn and put them where you tell him to," he said. "You shouldn't be lugging bags in your condition."

She shook her head and chuckled softly. "Harley, I never lug bags," she said, then she turned and waved her hand, lifting a display of supplements off the floor several feet.

Harley's eyes widened, and he nodded. "That's right," he said. "I guess I never get used to that kind of thing. But I still would like to take care of this for you."

She smiled at the old man who she knew was just trying to do something to make amends. "Thank you, Harley," she said. "That would make my life easier."

His smile widened. "Thank you, Hazel," he replied. "For giving me a chance."

When Hazel walked out of the store and walked back toward her truck, she saw Dustin waiting next to it.

"You went in there?" he asked, surprised. "Wasn't he the person who kidnapped you?"

She shrugged. "Yeah, but he seemed actually sorry he did it."

Dustin rolled his eyes. "Oh, well then, we should invite him home for dinner," he replied sarcastically. "Or maybe you could name the baby after him." He paused for a moment. "What's his name?"

"Harley," Hazel replied with a smile.

Dustin shook his head. "No. No grandchild of mine is going to be named after a motorcycle," he stated, then he winked at her. "Can I interest you in a donut or a sweet roll?"

Hazel's eyes widened. "Always," she said, slipping her hand through his. "And to what do I owe the honor of this meeting?"

"Well, your mother might have mentioned you were going to the feed store this morning when I called a little while ago," he said. "And I might have felt some overwhelming fatherly need to come and watch over you."

"I'm okay with overwhelming fatherly need," she replied with a smile. "Especially when baked goods are involved."

They walked over to a small bakery/café down the street from the feed store and placed their orders. They chatted about the weather and argued briefly about the benefits of living in Wisconsin over Colorado until their order was delivered to them at their small corner booth. When the waitress walked away, Dustin lowered his voice and leaned closer to Hazel.

"How did it go with him? Harley?" he asked.

"He was very humble, ashamed of what he did," she said, as she pulled off a piece of the cinnamon roll.

139

"He said that it was as if words were coming out of his mouth that weren't his."

Dustin shook his head. "So, it wasn't his fault, right?" he asked, disgusted.

She shook her head as she chewed. "No," she finally said. "He did say that some of the thoughts were his, so he couldn't blame everything on the demon. He said that things just got twisted up in his head. It sounds like he couldn't explain how he'd gotten where he was."

Dustin nodded slowly. "Frog soup."

"I beg your pardon," Hazel exclaimed softly, wrinkling her nose.

Chuckling softly, Dustin shook his head. "Not to eat," he said. "But an old story behind it."

"Is this like a wise dad story?" she teased.

"Exactly," he agreed with a grin. "So, the story goes that a farmer went out to his field and caught a whole burlap sack of frogs in order to make soup."

"Gross," Hazel inserted.

Dustin nodded, then continued, "He had a big pot of boiling water on the stove, just ready and waiting for those frogs. But when he dumped the sack full into the hot water, they all jumped right out of the water and hopped all over his kitchen."

"As they should have," she said, pulling off another piece of cinnamon roll.

"So, the farmer thought about it and decided that he had gone about this whole frog soup thing in the wrong way. He dumped out the hot water and set a large pan of nice cool water on the stove. Then he put the frogs in the cool water. They loved it; they didn't jump out at all. They swam around, enjoying themselves."

"So, what happens?" she asked.

"Then the farmer slowly turned up the heat, in tiny negligible amounts…"

"The farmer used the word negligible?" she teased.

"He was a very educated farmer," he replied. "Tiny amounts, that were barely noticeable. The water slowly got warmer, but the frogs didn't pay any attention to it, because they were slowly getting acclimated to the temperature change. Ten minutes later, frog soup."

"Gross, again," Hazel said. "But I understand what you're saying. The demon influenced Harley with small things at first, slowly getting him used to thinking that way, and pretty soon, Harley doesn't realize how far he's come from where he used to be."

Dustin nodded. "Right," he said. "If someone had first come to Harley and said I want you to kidnap Hazel, he would have turned them down flat. But slowly, compromise after compromise, they changed who Harley was."

Hazel sat back against the back of the booth and nodded slowly. "I would guess that probably has happened to a lot of people in this community," she said. "Makes me almost not want to hate them as much."

Dustin laughed and nodded. "There you go," he said. "I've totally changed your outlook on life."

She laughed too. "Well, you have given me something to think about," she agreed. "Not all of them are the enemy; some are as confused as Harley."

"Yes," Dustin agreed. "And when you don't respond with anger and hate, I think it confuses them. It might even make them reconsider their path in life." He sighed and shrugged. "And if we don't try to build bridges, who will they turn to when they realize that they don't want to serve the demon any longer?"

Chapter Twenty

Wanda Wildes adjusted her sunglasses before she walked into the box store on the outskirts of Whitewater. She pulled a cart from the long line near the front door and pushed it through the automatic glass doors. The produce section was to her left, and she pulled her cart next to the potato bin to scan the list Ben had given her. She could bet a hundred dollars that produce was not on the top of the list.

The men were lying low in a high-end log cabin about ten miles north of town. Wanda didn't ask Ben how he came to reserve a place like that mainly because she didn't want to know the answer. She shuddered as she thought back to the look on the young officer's face as Ben choked him to death. There was no reason for it, Ben did it because he could, and he could do it to any of them.

Taking a deep breath to steady herself, she pushed the cart away from the produce section and headed toward the back of the store where the frozen food, chips, and beer aisles were. She stopped at the bread aisle and glanced at the list. Hot dog buns and hamburger buns, they were going to grill, Wade had told her.

She turned down the aisle and immediately regretted it. Standing in the aisle about ten feet away from her was Hazel Willoughby, looking at the cheese crackers. She started to step backwards, but before she could get away, Hazel turned and looked at her.

Surprise was Hazel's first impression. What the hell was Wanda doing at the store? Then she chuckled at herself, duh, buying groceries. She quickly thought of her father's advice.

Nope, she thought decisively. I'm not going to be friends with Wanda.

Then a little voice in her head reminded her that being nice would really mess with Wanda's mind.

"Hey, Wanda," she said easily, picking up a family-sized box of cheddar-cheese snack crackers and putting them in her cart. "Please tell me that you didn't move my truck again." She placed her hand on her swollen belly and grimaced. "I don't have the energy to search for it today."

Wanda stared at her for a long moment before she replied. "No, I didn't touch your truck. Why are you even talking to me?" she asked, perplexed.

Hazel shrugged and bit back a grin. "I don't know," she said, "probably something my dad said to me. And it just seemed like the thing to do. I mean, we've known each other since before kindergarten."

"But you never liked me," Wanda insisted.

Hazel wasn't sure that was true. She actually remembered liking Wanda, a long time ago.

"No, that's not true, I remember inviting you to my birthday party in kindergarten," she said. "But you couldn't come."

"You remember that far back?" she replied, astonished.

This time Hazel let the grin appear. "Yeah, my sisters hate it," she admitted. "I can remember the most

146

random things. Anyway, we were friends up until then, and after my birthday, you didn't like me anymore."

"Being friends for half a year in kindergarten does not qualify as liking each other," Wanda replied, surprised she was enjoying the conversation.

"More than half a year," Hazel replied, feeling her anger ebb away. "My birthday's in April, so nearly the whole school year."

Wanda rolled her eyes but couldn't help but smile. "I really wanted to go to your party," she found herself confessing. "My parents wouldn't let me."

Nodding, Hazel smiled back. "Well, I was one of the weird Willoughbys," she said. "So, I'm not surprised."

"Why don't you hate me?" Wanda asked, sincerely confused by the conversation.

I have no idea, Hazel thought. No, that's not the right answer.

Hazel shrugged. "Because hate takes a lot of energy," she finally replied. "And I really don't have a lot of energy these days. Besides, I think you're as much a victim of fate as I am."

"I'm not a victim," Wanda snapped. "I have chosen…" She stopped as the memories of the day before flooded into her mind. Had she really chosen? Had she ever had a choice?

She looked up, the confusion evident in her face.

"Hey, I didn't mean to upset you," Hazel said, feeling a little guilty that she actually had wanted to mess with her mind. "I'll just go now. You have a great day, Wanda."

Then Hazel turned her cart around and walked away.

Wanda watched her, a mixture of confusion and regret fighting within her. Could she have been Hazel's friend? What would have happened if she had gone to that party so many years ago?

She shook her head. No, it was a trick. Hazel Willoughby was just playing some kind of mind game with her, that's all. Those bitches deserved what was coming to them.

Just like the young officer?

The question strayed into her thoughts.

"I just can't think about this right now," she whispered to herself. "I just need to do what I've been told."

She grabbed hold of the cart and pushed it forward. "Just do what you're told, Wanda," she whispered again. "And things will be fine."

Chapter Twenty-one

"Why ain't we waiting for Wanda?" Wade asked as he opened the shoebox that held brand new hiking boots. He reached over and grabbed a doughnut from the box on the kitchen counter. Wanda had picked up the doughnuts and some other meager supplies at a gas station the night before.

"Because we don't need her," Ben said, as he slipped into his camouflage jacket and slipped a pistol into the holster strapped across his chest.

"But she's bringing the beer," Wade replied, as he unlaced the rawhide shoestrings.

"It's not even noon," Ben snapped, turning to sneer at Wade. "You don't need beer."

"It's been months since I had a cold one," Buck inserted. "Wouldn't hurt nothing to bring some along on the hike."

"Shut the hell up," Ben yelled at both men. "Don't you realize what's at stake here? Don't you realize that we have been selected to serve the Master?"

"Well, yeah," Wade said with a casual shrug. "But, you know, we've got less than one week until Samhain. Nothing's going to happen 'til then."

"Right," Neal agreed. "We're just hanging out until then, right?"

"Wrong!" Ben yelled, clearing everything off the kitchen counter with a swipe of his arm. "Wrong! Wrong! Wrong?"

"Dude," Buck said, picking up a box of doughnuts. "There's no need to destroy everything."

But before he could place the box back on the counter, Ben had his hand around Buck's throat and was lifting him off the ground. "Don't you ever disrespect me, boy," he growled.

Choking, Buck could only stare at Ben and wheeze. Finally, Ben tossed him across the room and then turned to the other men who were staring at him in

151

disbelief. "The Master has given us a special assignment," he said, his voice low and threatening. "And if you don't do everything I tell you to do, you will die. Do you understand?"

Nodding mutely, the men stepped further away from Ben, picked up their hiking boots, and quickly began putting them on and lacing them up.

Ben turned to Buck, who was still on the floor next to the couch, rubbing his neck. "You," he growled, pointing at Buck. "You have already failed the Master once; you don't want to do it twice. Do you understand?"

Buck shook his head rapidly. "Yes, yes, sir," he stammered. "I do. I really do."

"You'd better," Ben replied. "Now, get ready."

Buck crawled across the room to get back to his equipment scattered on the floor. Ben watched him, a satisfied smirk on his face. "You've got three minutes to be ready," he said. "Then, we're leaving."

He walked to the front windows, their curtains closed tightly, and carefully moved the edge slightly so he could look outside. Their nearest neighbor was a mile away and was another rental cabin, so the likelihood of it being rented this late in the season was slim. He had insisted they not use lights, only flashlights pointed down, and they hadn't used the wood-burning stove. The driveway was dirt and covered with leaves. He'd insisted that Wanda stop on the road and not drive up to the house, so no one would see tire tracks. So far, it looked like their plan was going to work.

He smiled to himself. All he needed was to hide out for less than a week, then, everything would be his. The Master had promised him wealth, power, and prestige. He would rule alongside the greatest ruler this world would ever know. His smile widened. And if a few Willoughbys had to die to make that happen, so much the better.

"Did you give Wanda the extra key?" Ben barked out.

Wade nodded. "Yeah," he replied quickly. "I did just what you asked me to do. She's gonna get supplies, make sure she's not being tailed, then come on back here and drop off the stuff."

"Then she's leaving, right?" Ben asked.

"What?" Wade asked. "No. I mean, I figured she could stay…"

Ben glared at Wade. "And then she's leaving, right?" he stated emphatically.

It took only a moment for Wade to understand. "Yeah, right, okay," he said. "I'll leave her a note and tell her not to hang around."

"Good," Ben replied.

"You know, you can trust Wanda," Wade said. "She's one of us. Solid. To the bone."

"She's soft, and we can't depend on her," Ben said, shaking his head. "She's letting her emotions rule her. Typical woman. We don't need her screwing up our mission. We'll use her for supplies, but nothing else. You don't tell her nothing about what we're doing. Got it?"

Wade nodded. "Yeah, got it," he said, scribbling down a note and putting it on the counter. "Course, got it."

"Let's go," Ben said, pulling open the back door. "We've got a ways to hike."

"Where are we going?" Neal asked, hurrying to the door and grabbing a doughnut on the way out.

"To the lake," Ben said. "And the rock."

Chapter Twenty-two

"It's weird, isn't it?" Cat asked, as she and Donovan walked down the street towards his office in downtown Whitewater.

"What?" he asked, glancing over at her.

"Knowing that the world could end in less than a week," she said. "And walking down the street with all these people who have no idea of what's going on."

He chuckled humorlessly. "Yeah. And if we were to tell them, they'd think we were nuts," he agreed. "That can't happen to us. That can't happen here."

She nodded slowly. "I'd think the same thing if I wasn't smack dab in the middle of it," she agreed. Then she slowed and met his eyes. "Are we nuts?"

He turned to her, his eyes filled with regret. "Yes, we are," he said quietly. "Because if we were sane, we'd run away from all of this and spend as much time as we could together. Falling even more deeply in love."

"I don't think I could fall any more in love with you than I already am," she replied evenly, and then she sighed. "And I know that I would feel guilty if I left my family and my duty."

"And that's only one of the reasons I love you," he said. "Because you are loyal and brave."

"I don't really feel brave right now," she replied. "I think I would actually consider running away with you if I thought you were at all serious. But I know you, and you have never run away from a fight."

"So, back to our dilemma," he said with a sad smile. "What do we do with the time we have?"

She chewed on her lower lip for a moment, trying to decide if she should tell him what her family had discussed that morning.

"What?" he asked.

Her eyes widened in mock innocence. "What do you mean, what?" she asked, prevaricating.

"Catalpa Willoughby," he said sternly. "I have known you long enough to know that when you chew on

157

your adorable bottom lip, you are trying to decide whether or not to lie."

"I don't lie," she replied firmly. Then she smiled and shrugged easily. "Although I may not always offer all of the information."

"Tell me," he requested.

"My mother had a visitor last night," she began.

"Was it the demon?" he exclaimed urgently.

Cat shook her head. "No. No, nothing like that," she said, calming him. "Her mother, my grandmother, appeared to her. She gave her kind of a mom lecture and told her she needed to concentrate on the things that would bring joy."

"Isn't that what one of the sisters said?" Donovan asked.

"Yes, it was," she agreed. "But, you know, Mom has been worried about the burden she's placed on the three of us. She doesn't think it's fair."

"Well, it's not, actually," Donovan agreed. "But that wasn't a decision she made. It was made for all of you a hundred years ago."

"Exactly," Cat agreed. "And Mom had to sacrifice quite a bit herself."

"I thought about that when I saw her with Finias," he replied. "I don't think I could have done what Finias did if it had been you and me. I couldn't have walked away from you and our child. I couldn't have let you go."

She reached up and stroked his chin. "I don't think I could have done it either," she agreed. "But that had been impressed on her since she was old enough to understand. It was her…"

"Duty," Donovan finished. "So, how did your grandmother suggest she concentrate on joy?"

"Handfasting," Cat replied softly.

"Handfasting?" he repeated. "As in getting married."

Cat nodded. "She suggested that we, all three couples, get handfasted on Samhain. What do you think?"

"What do I think?" he repeated. He reached down, took Cat's hand in his, brought it to his lips, and kissed it reverently, gazing into her eyes over her hand. "I think that's a brilliant idea. I would feel much better, knowing that we are bound together when we face the demon."

"Are you sure?" she asked, worried that she was pushing him into something he really didn't want to do.

Then he lifted the hand he was holding and placed it on the side of his head. "Cat read my thoughts," he said. "And you tell me if I'm sure."

She closed her eyes and linked herself to him. Suddenly, she felt the love and the passion he felt for her like a giant wave pulsing over her. The emotions were so powerful and intense that she was overcome. She felt her knees buckle, but before she could fall, Donovan had wrapped his arms around her and pulled her against him.

"What did you see, Cat," he demanded hotly into her ear.

She trembled in his arms. "You love me," she said, her voice breathy and awestruck. "You love me so much."

"Yes," he whispered in her ear, still holding her close. "Yes, I do."

Chapter Twenty-three

Agnes wiped down the last countertop, placed the dish towel over a rod near the sink, turned, and leaned back against the sink gazing at the room. Small containers of calendula ointment were stacked on the table, waiting for Cat to label them and bring them into the store's warehouse area. A vase overflowing with mums and dried grasses was on the table, a gift from Rowan. Hazel's leather chore gloves were on the corner of the counter, where she always left them. Signs of life, her daughters' lives, were everywhere. She had been given a good life, she needed to remember that, she reminded herself, as the next few days progressed.

She turned on the television in the kitchen, planning to catch up on the news while she washed the dishes in the sink. She turned away from the screen to put dishwashing liquid into the sink when a special news bulletin was announced.

"Authorities from Iron County Prison have announced the escape of four fugitives. Ben Stoughton, Wade Wildes, and Neal and Buck Abbott escaped last night from the prison. Area residents are asked to be on the lookout for these men. If you see them, do not try to apprehend them. They should be considered armed and dangerous."

The bottle of dishwashing liquid slipped from her shaking hands, and she took a deep breath. She instantly remembered the dream she'd had before her mother's visit and her mother's words before she had gone to the football game that night.

"I just taught you the most important lesson of life," she said, her eyes somber and truthful. "If you can remember this when hard times come and when life presents its challenges, I have done my job. Find joy, my dear sweet Agnes, always find joy."

She closed her eyes in despair and wondered what her mother would have done if she'd known the truth of what had happened that night. If her mother would have been able to keep the oath of "an harm it none," if she had known what had happened between Ben Stoughton and her daughter.

Agnes parked her car in the high school parking lot and hurried across the street to the stadium gate, where her friends had agreed to meet her.

"You made it!" her best friend, Stephanie, squealed with excitement. "Your mom actually let you come!"

"She was so cool about it," Agnes replied. "She told me that I was supposed to have fun in my life."

"This is so great," Stephanie replied. "Come on, we still have time to grab some food and get our seats before the kickoff."

They paid their entrance fee and hurried over to the concession stand. There was a crowd in front of the stand, and they selected one of the lines to wait in.

"What are you going to get?" Stephanie asked.

Agnes shrugged; she really hadn't been exposed to a lot of junk food. "Maybe a hot dog," she suggested. "And some chips."

Stephanie nodded eagerly. "Good choices," she said. "And make sure you get a drink too. Their hot dog buns can be a little dry."

"Thanks," Agnes replied, immediately reconsidering her choice. "I'll remember that."

As they neared the window to place their order, Agnes heard someone cry out. She immediately turned and looked around. "What's that?" she asked.

Stephanie shrugged. "Stuff sometimes happens behind the concession stand," she said, lowering her voice.

"Stuff?" Agnes asked. "What kind of stuff?"

"You know, making out kind of stuff," her friend replied. "It's kind of secluded back there."

Agnes heard a muffled cry again. "That doesn't sound good," she said.

Stephanie nodded slowly. "Yeah, but we should stay out of it," she said. "It's none of our business."

"What? Why should we stay out of it?" she asked.

"You don't understand," Stephanie said, lowering her voice. "Those boys, they have like powers. I don't understand how, but they can do things to people."

"And those boys, they do things to girls?" Agnes asked, feeling her blood begin to boil.

"Yeah," she said, tears filling her eyes. "Yeah, they do things to girls."

"Have they done things to you?" Agnes asked.

The tears spilled from Stephanie's eyes and trailed down her cheeks. "It wasn't too bad," she said. "And they only did it once. They said they wouldn't hurt me as long as I never told anyone."

"I'll be right back," Agnes said, turning and heading toward the side of the concession stand.

"No," Stephanie called after her. "Please don't go."

Agnes glanced back over her shoulder. "I have to," she replied.

She jogged along the side of the concession stand and turned the corner. She could hear noise coming from the old bleachers that were stored behind the stand.

"Shut up," someone growled. "You know you want this."

Agnes ran towards the voice. She ran between the sets of bleachers and up the darkened passageway. Back underneath the bleachers, hidden by the outside wall of the school, Ben, Neal, and Wade were struggling with a girl. Her blouse was torn, and her jeans had been pulled down to her knees. Wade and Neal were holding her down and Ben was beginning to climb on top of her. She cried out again and Ben drew back and slapped her.

"I told you to shut up," he said.

"Ben Stoughton," Agnes yelled. "You get off of her immediately."

Ben turned and glared at Agnes. "What? You want a turn, Willoughby?" he sneered and licked his thick lips. "You want to take her place?"

Agnes felt nausea pool in her throat, and she was grateful she hadn't purchased the hot dog. She took a deep breath. "Now," she commanded.

Ben reached forward and slid his hand over the girl's exposed flesh. "And who's gonna stop me?" he asked.

The young girl's eyes were filled with a combination of revulsion and fear, and Agnes felt anger burn inside of her. "I guess I will," she said, her jaw clenched with determination.

She pointed at Ben and then waved her arm in the direction of the school. Instantly he was thrown off the girl and tossed against the brick wall. Then she looked at Wade and Neal. "Move! Now!" she demanded.

Both boys jumped up and ran away from the girl, towards the other side of the bleachers.

"Get back here," Ben demanded, stumbling away from the wall. *"We can take her."*

Agnes turned and faced him. "No, you can't," she said.

Ben stared at her for a moment, a wicked smile on his face. "Oh, yes, we can," he said. *He lifted his hands in front of him, and then moved them closer, mimicking the movement of clasping them around her neck. Agnes immediately felt the pressure on her neck, cutting off her air.*

"Great trick, right?" he sneered, slowly moving towards her.

She gasped, bringing her hands to her throat.

"Yeah, Willoughby, you think you're so tough," he stated with satisfaction. *"You are nothing compared to me."*

Agnes turned to the girl, who sat wide-eyed and terrified. "Run," Agnes gasped.

The girl scrambled to her feet and ran away.

"She's not going for help. She's not coming back here," Ben crowed, as he stepped up to Agnes. *"She's too afraid to snitch on me. She can see what I can do."*

Agnes' vision began to blur, and she knew she didn't have much time before she would be unconscious.

Ben laughed. "But don't worry, you can take her place. Once you pass out, the boys and I are going to have a little fun with you,"

He moved his hand from its clenched position in order to run it down her shirt and squeeze her breast. "I'm gonna enjoy boning you, Willoughby," he sneered.

Agnes gasped for air, even as she felt her skin crawl with revulsion at his touch. She had never had sex; she hadn't even gotten close. Because of her part in the spell, she knew when she had sex, it was vital to be sure her partner shared the same values and attributes of her own coven.

She couldn't let someone as crude and vulgar as Ben have a chance at becoming the father of one of the three. Power, white and hot, surged through her. She

170

swiped her hand to the side and threw Ben several feet away from her.

"Hey!" he exclaimed. "Dudes! Get her. Hold her down."

She turned to Wade and Neal and, with another wave of her hand, tossed them easily aside.

Ben stood up and started to charge her. But she threw her hand to the side, and Ben crashed against the backsides of bleacher steps. He dropped to the sandy soil beneath and turned towards her. "No one does that to me," he screamed. "No one!"

He reached up and felt the blood streaming from his nose, then scrambled to his feet, his face contorted in anger.

"You can't..." he began.

Still filled with fury, she waved her hand again and sent him flying into the bleachers once more. She heard the crack of bone against wood, and this time when he dropped to the ground, he didn't get up.

"You killed him," Wade screamed from the edge of the bleachers. "You killed him."

Immediately, Agnes felt the anger fade and a sickening dread blossom in the pit of her stomach. She moved forward and studied Ben's inert body. Finally, she knelt down next to him and could feel that his life force was slowly ebbing away.

"An harm it none," she whispered, disgusted by her actions. She realized that her first acts were self-preservation, but then she had allowed anger and hatred towards this boy who had bullied her all her young life to rule her actions. But there was no excuse for what she'd done, and now, she'd have to make amends.

Laying her hands on his shoulders, she closed her eyes and tried to remember what her mother had taught her about human anatomy. She searched through Ben's internal organs, his muscles, and finally found the break in his neck and the damage to his spinal cord. Concentrating all of her power, she went to work repairing the damaged spinal column and then repairing

172

and realigning his vertebra. After ten minutes, Agnes

opened her eyes and inhaled deeply. Sweat was running

down her forehead, and her hands were shaking from

exhaustion. She grabbed onto the bleachers and pulled

herself up, then stumbled away from Ben.

"Is he dead?" Neal asked, inching forward.

Agnes shook her head. "No," she gasped. "No,

he'll live."

"We're gonna sue you," Wade challenged.
"We're gonna sue you for attempted murder."

"Yeah, we're gonna call the cops and have you

arrested," Neal added.

Agnes turned and looked at them, too tired to even

be amused. "And who is going to believe you?" she asked,

disgusted. "Take him home. He's going to need rest."

They ran over and lifted up their friend, who was

just beginning to regain consciousness. Ben opened his

eyes and looked at Agnes. "I was dead..." he stammered.

She shrugged. "No, only almost dead," she said.

"You killed me," he breathed. "You killed me."

"And I brought you back," Agnes snapped.
"Don't make me regret my choice."

For the first time ever, Agnes saw fear in Ben's eyes.

"Let's get out of here," he said to Wade and Neal. "Let's get out of here now."

Agnes leaned against the bleachers and watched them leave. Then she dropped to the ground and wept grateful tears that her hands weren't stained with Ben's blood.

Agnes picked up the bottle of dishwashing liquid and squirted it into the sink, as the memory faded away and the news bulletin continued. "We repeat, these men should be considered armed and dangerous."

Agnes looked at the mugshots of them on the television and noted Ben's sneer, not unlike the sneer he'd worn in high school. She lifted up the remote, pointed it at the television, and changed the channel.

"An harm it none," she whispered, putting the remote back on the countertop, "unless he tries to hurt one of my own."

She lifted up her phone and tapped in a number, then she put the phone to her ear. "Hello, Finias," she said a moment later. "Something's happened, and we all need to meet, right away."

Chapter Twenty-four

Wanda drove around the backroads for fifteen extra minutes, just to be sure she wasn't followed. She knew it wouldn't be long before they connected her with the escape of her father and the other men, she'd been at the prison on the day they'd escaped. She ground her teeth in frustration. Why hadn't they waited? Why hadn't they taken the explosives from her and waited another couple of days? That's what she had suggested. But Ben had other plans, Ben always had other plans.

Slowing her car at the intersection, she checked her rearview mirror one more time. Then she rolled down her window and checked the skies for drones, she knew she couldn't be too cautious. Finally, she turned right and drove down the narrow dirt road to the cabin. She drove past the driveway and parked several yards up the road. Then she got out of her car, opened the trunk, and levitated all of the bags inside. With a wave of her hand, the bags moved away from the car, so she could close the trunk, then she walked alongside her purchases through the tree line to the back of the cabin.

Fishing the key from her purse, she unlocked the garage door and stepped inside. The garage was empty except for some equipment hanging from hooks on the walls. The concrete floor was swept clean, even the ladders, gardening equipment, shovels, and brooms were neatly stashed on special hangers attached to the walls.

She walked across the area, bags floating alongside her, and opened the door to the interior of the house. "Hello," she called. "I've got the groceries."

When there was no answer, she directed the packages to the counters. Once settled, she started unpacking them, putting the refrigerated items away first and then storing the rest in the small closet pantry in the kitchen. It wasn't until she was folding up the bags that she saw the scribbled note from her father laying on the counter.

"You don't need to stay here. Dad"

She picked the note up and enclosed it within her fist. Then she closed her eyes and let the impressions open up to her. She could see the room, with the men getting ready for their hike. She saw that Ben was impatient and angry. She concentrated on him and could finally pick up what he was saying.

"She's soft, and we can't depend on her. She's letting her emotions rule her. Typical woman. We don't need her screwing up our mission. We'll use her for supplies, but nothing else. You don't tell her nothing about what we're doing. Got it?"

"So, where are you going?" she wondered aloud.

Walking to the back door, she placed her hand on the doorknob and closed her eyes once again. She could feel Ben's imprint on the door, and she concentrated on the thoughts he was having as he stood there. She could see the path he was planning to take and followed them in her mind.

"Why is he going to the campground?" she whispered, confused. "There's going to be at least a few campers there. They're going to get caught."

With a frustrated sigh, she lifted her hand from the doorknob and stepped back. Then she hurried over to the pantry and pulled out paper towels and cleaning spray. She walked back and sprayed the doorknob, wiping it carefully to remove her fingerprints. She did the same to any surface she touched, including the groceries.

"You want to get caught, fine," she murmured as she worked. "But you're not going to pull me into your mess."

Placing the cleaning spray back into the pantry, she quickly wiped it down. Then she picked up the grocery bags and the used paper towels and took them with her as she exited the house. She pulled her shirt over her hand when she used the key, then left the key under a planter behind the house.

"You'll be safe there," she said. "And I'll be safe not carrying it with me."

She jogged away from the house, back to the tree line, and hurried to her car. Stopping at the edge of the woods, she froze when she heard another car coming up the road. In dismay, she realized that her license plate would be easily discernable where she was parked. She glanced up the road and saw that the car hadn't reached the bend. With a quick flick of her hand, she splattered mud from the small creek next to the car onto the body, including the license plate. The mud disguised not only the plate but also the color of the small car.

Backing into the woods, she hid behind a large oak until the car had driven past her. Then she waited until she could no longer hear it. Finally, she cleaned her car off with another quick wave of her hand and slipped inside.

Seated inside, she placed her hands on the steering wheel and exhaled softly. She realized that she didn't want to be part of this anymore. She was tired of being taken for granted. Tired of being used as a pawn in someone else's intrigue.

She thought about the moment at the grocery store with Hazel and her heart filled with regret. She didn't want to feel hate anymore. She didn't give a damn about the Master, she just wanted things to go back to the way they were.

Putting her key in the ignition, she started her car.

"I just hope they don't do something stupid," she muttered, then she shifted into drive and pulled away.

Chapter Twenty-five

Ben held up his hand to warn the men behind him to stop walking. They froze in their tracks and stared at each other, too frightened to speak. Ben moved forward on the narrow deer path and stopped at the edge of the woods, looking down at the small public campsite below.

A compact car was parked in the lot adjacent to the wooded campsite, a small two-person tent was set up about ten yards away from it, in a small clearing, and various camping paraphernalia was scattered on the wooden picnic table several feet away from the tent. A rope clothesline was strung between two trees and two large bath towels hung from it. Smoke was still curling up from the firepit near the picnic table, and the two pairs of hiking boots sitting outside the tent made it clear that the occupants of the site were still there.

Ben turned to the rest of the group. "We've got to move quickly," he said, then he looked at them pointedly. "And quietly."

"What are we gonna do?" Wade asked.

"We're gonna get ourselves some volunteers," Ben replied, his voice low and threatening.

"I don't understand," Neal said. "What are they volunteering to do?"

Ben looked over at Neal, disgust in his expression. "They're going to volunteer to be human sacrifices so the Master can increase his strength," he said pointedly.

"We're going to kill them?" Wade asked, astonished.

"No," Ben said and smirked when he saw the relief on the faces of the two older men. "Not until we get them to the rock."

He turned to Buck. "I want you to go down there first," he said. "Act like you're lost and looking for directions."

Buck nodded. "Yes, sir," he replied.

"Make sure you're standing with your back to the road, so we can sneak up behind them," Ben added. Then he turned to the other two men. "As soon as they walk out

183

of their tent and start talking to Buck, I'll take care of catching them. I want you two to take care of their equipment and their car. Got it?"

The two men nodded mutely.

"I don't want nothing to go wrong here," Ben growled. "Or I just might have to substitute some of you in their place."

Wade swallowed audibly and nodded. Neal just slowly nodded, his eyes wide with fright.

Ben turned back to Buck. "Okay, go now," he said. "And make sure you don't do anything that makes them suspicious. Don't go looking over their shoulders to watch us."

"Yes, sir," he replied, his throat dry. "I'll make sure they don't know what hit them."

Buck stayed inside the tree line until he was situated in front of their tent, then he slowly made his way down the hill toward their campsite. When he got closer to the tent, he stopped and called out, "Hello! Hello! Is anyone around?"

Instantly there was movement inside the tent, and a few moments later, a young man dressed in jeans and a flannel shirt poked his head out from between the tent flaps.

"Hey, what's up?" he called.

Buck walked down a little further, getting closer to the tent. "Hey, sorry to disturb you," he said. "But I am totally lost. I took some path, and I got turned around."

The young man climbed out of the tent and stood up. His feet were shod in thick wool socks, and he motioned to the picnic table. "I've got a map over here in my stuff," he offered. "Why don't we take a look."

"Hey, thanks," Buck said, walking over to the table, but staying on the side closest to the street. "Where are you from?"

"Chicago," the young man replied. "My wife and I try to escape every chance we can."

"Wow, Chicago," Buck replied. "Must be crazy crowded there."

A young woman climbed out of the tent next to them. "It is," she said with a smile. "Which is why we're up here in this beautiful place." She turned to her husband. "Even though we nearly froze our butts off last night."

She walked over to stand next to her husband. "So, are you from around here?" she asked.

Buck paused for a moment. He knew he couldn't tell them that he was from Whitewater because it would be hard to explain getting lost. But, for the life of him, he couldn't think of any other town.

They both stared at him suspiciously, and the young man placed his hand protectively around his wife's shoulders.

"Hey, sorry," Buck finally said. "I was trying to think of a place to tell you instead of admitting that I'm from Whitewater and I'm lost in my own backyard." He finished his explanation with an embarrassed shrug. "But, I guess, other than being lost, I'm also really bad at coming up with new town names out of the blue."

The young couple laughed and nodded. "I totally get that," she said. "I've gotten lost in Chicago, and I hate to admit it."

"She's worse than I am about asking directions," her husband teased.

Buck laughed. "I hate that too," he said. "If you guys had been a gas station, I would have never asked."

As they all laughed at his comment, a sudden wind blew through the campsite, intensifying in strength as it continued.

"Whoa, this is unexpected," he said, shouting over the wind.

"The weather app said it was supposed to be nice today," his wife replied, looking up at the sky.

Suddenly, the rope and towels from between the trees became unlashed and flew through the air towards them. The towels slapped into their faces, but before they could pull them off, the rope wrapped around their bodies, pinning their arms to their sides and securing the towels in place.

"Help us," the young man cried out. "Cut the rope."

"Please help us," the woman cried out, struggling to get free.

Buck shrugged. "Sorry," he said. "But you probably should have stayed in Chicago."

Any response they might have made was halted when Ben hit them in the head with the butt of his gun, and they dropped to the ground.

Chapter Twenty-six

"So, what's up?" Hazel asked as she walked into the great room with several large bags. "I brought food."

The rest of the group was already gathered around the big oak table.

Rowan laughed. "Well, of course, you did,' she said. "What did you get?"

"Sandwiches, chips, cookies," she replied, then she grinned. "Brownies, donuts, and there might even be some pie in there." She glanced over and smiled at her mom. "I warned you not to send the pregnant one."

"What? No, pickles?" Cat teased.

"Oh, yes, thanks for reminding me," Hazel said. "The dill pickle in there is mine."

Joseph stood up and pulled out a chair next to his, then he took the bags from her. "I saved this chair for you," he said. "Have a seat, I'll pass out the food."

Hazel sat down and looked over at her mom. "Do you want to start before we eat?" she asked.

"Well, my information won't take that long to deliver," Agnes replied. "I think the longer conversation will be what we're going to do about it."

"What's up, darling?" Seamus asked.

"I just learned from a news report that Ben Stoughton, Wade Wildes, and Neal and Buck Abbott have escaped from prison," she stated evenly, even though her hands were shaking. "They escaped yesterday, and no one knows where they are."

Silence fell around the table as everyone absorbed the information. Donovan turned to Joseph. "Did they let you know?" he asked.

Joseph shook his head. "No, they didn't," he replied, then he paused. "But then again, I'm not sure how many of Stoughton's minions still work at the department. We could have received something, and it got 'filed" before I could see it."

"They're coming back here," Cat said. "We have to assume that they're coming back here."

Agnes nodded. "That makes the most sense," she agreed.

"Why? Why would that make the most sense?" Henry asked. "They escaped from prison. Why would they want to go back to the first place everyone would be looking for them?"

"To serve the demon," Donovan said. "They have probably been promised riches and power."

"And that's something that Ben Stoughton could never turn down," Agnes added.

"I saw Wanda at the grocery store today," Hazel inserted slowly. "She had a couple of cases of beer in her cart. I thought it was kind of strange because Wanda has always been a white wine kind of person."

"What else did she have?" Joseph asked. "If you can remember."

Hazel turned and smiled at her fiancé. "Actually, it was filled with junk food," she said. "I remember looking at it and feeling jealous."

"Beer and junk food," Donovan said. "That sounds more like the kind of food Ben, Wade, Neal, and Buck would eat, not Wanda."

Rowan remembered her last encounter with Buck and shivered. Henry turned to her and put his arm around her shoulders. "Don't worry," he said, his voice low. "He will not hurt you again."

She took a deep breath. "Well, at least we're forewarned," she said softly. "And we also need to set up some kind of watch on the house."

"Tell me," Finias said. "What did these men do? Why were they jailed?"

"They were jailed because of drugs," Hazel said, reaching for a wrapped sandwich and putting it on her plate. "Drugs that Donovan planted on them, so they'd go to jail."

"What they really did was shoot Henry and nearly kill him," Cat added. "Then they tried to kidnap him when we went to the hospital."

"And then Buck broke into my Still Room and assaulted me because he thought we had a secret the demon wanted," Rowan said.

"And when Henry saw what Buck had done to Rowan, he suddenly remembered how to use his powers," Agnes added. "He made sure Buck paid for what he did to Rowan."

"So, they know of your powers and your strengths?" Finias asked, then he turned to Donovan. "And do they know that you are the one who betrayed them."

Donovan shook his head. "I don't think they know it was me," he said. "Although I wasn't as careful as I could have been. I didn't anticipate them breaking out."

"But they haven't been around for months," Hazel said. "So, they don't know what's happened since. They don't know about Joseph. Or about Donovan coming back to the right side."

Donovan turned and snatched a chip from Hazel's plate. "Hey, I've always been on the right side," he said to

193

her. "I just pretended to be on their side to protect all of you."

"Will they know you're on our side?" Finias asked.

Cat shook her head. "Yes, they have a lot of contacts in town," she said. "I'm sure word has gotten out of our last encounter with the coven."

Finias turned to Agnes. "This is your home," he said. "And you need to make the final decisions. But I would suggest that we all stay here, so we are a united force."

Agnes nodded. "I agree," she said. "There's less than one week until Samhain. If they are working with the demon, they are going to be desperate to stop us."

"We can work out shifts for guard duty," Joseph added.

"Guard duty?" Dustin asked. "Isn't the house already protected?"

"The last time this group decided to go after us, they shot Henry with a high-powered rifle from the road,"

194

Rowan said. "They don't always use witchcraft to do their dirty work."

"Well, then," Seamus said, rubbing his hands together happily. "Where's me gun, and who do I get to shoot?"

"Have you ever used a firearm before?" Joseph asked him.

Seamus shrugged. "Well, no, but how hard can it be?" he asked.

"Target practice, starting tomorrow," Joseph said. "No one gets a gun until I'm comfortable with their abilities."

"Great!" Hazel said. "And since we're all going to be together, we can all plan the handfasting too."

"Handfasting?" several male voices questioned.

Hazel's eyes widened as she looked around the table and realized the only man who hadn't questioned it was Donovan. "Oops," she said, biting her lip in dismay. "Guess I let the cat out of the bag."

Chapter Twenty-seven

Finias opened the back door quietly and just stood in the doorway watching Agnes. She was gazing out over the pastures beyond the house, something he remembered her doing when they were married. She had told him it brought her peace. He wondered if it still brought her peace in these turbulent times.

"You look very thoughtful," he said, finally stepping out of the house and joining her on the back deck.

She quickly turned and smiled at him, although he could tell the smile was forced. "You do that very well," she replied.

"Do what?" he asked, coming towards her.

"Sneak up on me," she replied, her eyebrow arched as he moved closer.

"Do you mind if I come out here?" he asked. "Or would you rather be alone?"

She sighed softly and shook her head. "I was hoping that being alone for a few minutes would help me clear my thoughts," she admitted. "But they are no clearer now than they were ten minutes ago."

"Can I help?" he asked.

She looked up into his piercing blue eyes that seem to focus only on her with extraordinary intensity and shook her head again. "Finias, having you this close to me does nothing to help clear my thoughts."

He chuckled softly, then cradled her face in his hands. "I never forgot how beautiful you were," he said softly, lightly rubbing his thumbs along the soft skin of her jaw. "But, my memory did not do you justice."

She smiled at him, feeling the warmth spread through her body. "That's very sweet," she said, keeping her voice light in an effort to tamp down the emotions that were swirling within her. "But I do realize that I'm now a woman who has had three daughters and will soon be a grandmother. I am certainly not the same girl I was when we met."

He shook his head. "No, you are better," he replied sincerely. "You have grown into the beauty that was just on the surface when I met you. You have become more serene, more graceful, and wiser. Your smile reaches your heart and your eyes. Your compassion and understanding guide your words. The girl I loved was beautiful, but the woman who stands before me, she is exquisite."

He bent down again and brushed his lips against hers, tasting, teasing, and tempting. And waiting. Waiting for Agnes to not only acknowledge her desire for him but to act on it. He tasted her again and then left her mouth, sampling the tender skin of her jawline and her neck. She moaned softly, but stood still, a captive, not a participant.

"Agnes," he whispered, his voice filled with tension. "Show me how you feel."

He brought his lips back to hers, lightly teasing and tempting with soft open-mouthed caresses. Her breathing increased, and she gasped when he gently nibbled on her bottom lip and then laved the spot with his tongue.

Finally, it was too much for her. With a soft cry, Agnes threw her arms around his neck and pulled him closer. His hands slipped down from her face and embraced her tightly while his lips crushed hers, and his explorations deepened.

She was being swept away in a whirlwind of emotions. Her body was burning with need as her hands stroked his back, his neck, and then pulled him even closer. Their bodies fit together as if they had never separated. As if they had been carved by the same sculptor, ebony and ivory, to fit perfectly as one.

His hand slipped up, over her hip, up to her waist, and then tugged her blouse out of her jeans. She felt his hands on the bare skin of her waist and froze.

Finias immediately stopped and, after a moment, leaned back to meet her eyes. "Too much?" he asked, his voice hoarse.

She nodded slowly, gasping softly for air. "I can't believe..." she began.

He smiled tenderly. "That we nearly made love on your deck?" he asked.

"Finias!" she exclaimed. "I would never..."

He laughed and shook his head. "Oh, yes, my dear, actually, as I recall, we have," he teased. "And it was magical."

She stepped back to give herself a little breathing space.

"I'm a mother of three," she argued. "I don't just make love in the middle of the day in the middle of my backyard."

He stepped closer and met her eyes. "We could always go to your bedroom," he suggested.

Yes, she thought desperately. *Yes. Yes. Yes.*

"No," she said aloud. "I..."

"I want you," Finias said, his voice low. "I have never stopped wanting you."

She closed her eyes and sighed, holding her hand out defensively. "Please," she pleaded. "Just…"

But he didn't want her to put the barrier up between them ever again. He stepped forward and grasped the hand she was holding out, then brought it to his lips and pressed a slow, moist kiss on her palm. She gasped and opened her eyes, transfixed by the passion she saw within his eyes. "I haven't…" she whispered, her voice shaking slightly. "I haven't…since Hazel."

He slowly straightened, still holding her hand loosely in his own, and cocked his head to the side. "Since Hazel?" he asked, surprised.

She shook her head quickly, feeling embarrassed. "No," she said, looking anywhere but his searching eyes. "Really, it's no big deal. I was raising kids…"

He released her hand and crossed his arms over his chest. "Agnes," he said softly. "The truth."

With a shuddering sigh, she finally turned to him, tears glistening in her eyes. "I loved you," she said, her voice low and trembling. "No one else…after my duty had been done…it just didn't seem right."

He inhaled softly, amazed by the depth of love he still had for her too. "Agnes," he breathed, stepping closer to cradle her face in his hands. "Agnes…"

Noises filtered out to them through the kitchen window. Agnes felt her cheeks burn with humiliation. Her daughters were only yards away, and she was acting like…

"Agnes," Finias said, interrupting her thoughts. "Tell me about the handfasting."

She took a deep breath and nodded. "My mother came to me," she said.

"Your mother came to you? When?" Finias asked.

"Last night," she said with a sigh. "I was going to mention it to you. My mother suggested that the girls get handfasted before we meet the demon. So, the couples are bound together."

"That is a good idea," Finias agreed. "There is nothing more powerful than love." He saw her hesitate, so he brought her hand back up to his lips and kissed the top of her hand quickly. "Go on. I know there's more."

She couldn't meet his eyes, so she gently pulled her hand out of his grasp and turned to look out over the backyard. "The girls thought," she began. "It was all their idea. But the girls suggested that I should join them. Because, you know, four of the Willoughby women and their partners. Makes sense, right?"

Finias' smile slowly spread across his face as he watched her avoid eye contact with him. "It makes perfect sense," he agreed.

She shook her head, her hands clenched on the railing. "I'm so sorry. This is ridiculous," she stammered. "I don't want you to feel in any way obligated…"

She froze when Finias put his hand on her shoulder. Gently he turned her around and then knelt before her, taking her hand in his own. "Agnes Willoughby," he said tenderly, his eyes radiating his love.

"Will you do me the very great honor of becoming my wife, once again?"

She nodded, her eyes overflowing with tears.

"Yes," she cried softly. "Of course, yes, I will."

Chapter Twenty-eight

"Okay, that's adorable," Hazel said, peering through the kitchen window at her mother and Finias.

"What?" Rowan asked, wiping the last plate and placing it in the cabinet.

"Finias is proposing to Mom," Hazel replied.

"What?" Rowan exclaimed, hurrying over to the window. She wiped a tear from her cheek and smiled. "Oh, wow. Just wow."

Cat came into the kitchen, amused to see her sisters staring out the window together like they were both still in grade school. "What's up?" she asked.

"Finias is proposing to Mom," Rowan said. "And it's so sweet."

Cat rushed forward and peered over their heads to the deck just in time to see Finias pull Agnes into his arms and kiss her. "He's got some moves," Cat said, with more than a little pride for her father. Then she saw him deepen the kiss. "And maybe we need to give them a little privacy."

"Good idea," Hazel said, backing away and grinning. "I'm too impressionable to see much more of that."

"So, I'm guessing that means they're going to be participating in the handfasting," Cat said, as they three sat down at the kitchen table. "How about you two?"

Rowan shrugged. "I haven't exactly talked to Henry about it," she confessed. "It's kind of awkward."

Cat nodded. "I agree," she said. "But Donovan took it well." Her smile widened. "He took it very well."

Hazel leaned forward in her chair. "Oh, do tell," she teased.

Cat shook her head. "I do not kiss and tell," she said, and then she sighed softly. "But, yeah, it was great."

Hazel stood up. "Okay, then," she said, slapping her hand on the table. "I'm going for it. I need something to brighten up my day."

Rowan nodded. "I guess there's no time like the present," she agreed. "Perhaps Henry and I can take a walk to the Still Room."

Hazel and Cat glanced at the back door and smiled. "Make sure you use the front door," Hazel suggested, waggling her eyebrows.

Rowan laughed. "Yeah, good idea."

Hazel walked into the great room where the rest of the men were discussing security measures and leaned over the chair where Joseph was sitting. She bent over and wrapped her arms around his neck, "Hey, handsome," she said. "Want to walk me to the barn?"

He turned to the side, kissed her cheek, and nodded. "Sure," he said.

"Thanks," she replied, straightening up.

He got out of his chair and began to walk toward the kitchen, but Hazel grabbed his hand and nodded in the direction of the front door. "This way," she said.

"Why?" he asked.

She grinned. "I'll tell you later."

Hand in hand, they walked through the room and out the front door.

"They make a lovely couple," Seamus said, and then he turned to Rowan. "And you say he turns into a werewolf?"

Rowan sat down next to Henry on the couch and nodded to her father. "Fangs and all," she said. "But, it's closer to a skinwalker, because he can change when he wants to."

"And how does that work?" Seamus asked.

Henry leaned forward. "Well, actually, it's really quite fascinating," he began. "Rowan and I compared Joseph's DNA with the DNA found in the Canis lupus lupus, the Eurasian wolf, which, although not the largest wolf in the world it has the closest territory to where Joseph's ancestors came from…"

Rowan placed her hand on Henry's arm to interrupt him for a moment. "Darling, I hate to interrupt you," she said. "But there is something urgent that needs to be tended to in the Still Room, and I would really like for you to come with me."

"Of course," Henry said immediately. He turned to Seamus. "You don't mind if we continue this discussion later, do you?"

Seamus shook his head. "No, laddie, go with Rowan now. And take good care of her."

Henry stood up and offered his hand to Rowan to help her to her feet. "Oh, I intend to," he promised.

He started to walk toward the kitchen, but she stopped him and shook her head. "I'm afraid that we need to go out the front door too," she said, and when he looked confused, she smiled. "And I'll explain later too."

Chapter Twenty-nine

Joseph pulled the barn door closed behind them and leaned back against it. "So, what do we need to talk about?" he asked, crossing his arms over his chest.

"How do you know we need to talk?" Hazel asked, walking over to a stack of hay bales and sitting on them.

"Because you, my amazing Hazel, are so competent that everything having to do with the care and feeding of your goats is done by the time the sun rises," he teased. "So, out with it."

"What do you know about handfasting?" she asked, trying to sound casual.

He pushed himself away from the door and walked over to her. "Yeah, I was going to ask you about that," he said. "I don't have a clue."

"It's a Celtic tradition," she said. "You know how a handshake is often considering sealing a deal, it's along those same lines. A handfast is creating a contract or a promise. I'm sure Henry could give you a lot more details."

He leaned forward and placed a kiss on the top of her head. "Is that a roundabout way of saying it's a Celtic marriage ceremony?" he whispered.

She raised her head and looked into his eyes. "Sort of," she whispered back. "My grandmother thought it would be a good thing to do."

"Your grandmother is dead," he replied.

Hazel shrugs. "Yeah, but I guess that didn't stop her from visiting Mom last night," she said easily. "She told her that we needed to find joy in our lives. That it would make us all more powerful for Samhain."

He bent down and kissed her forehead. "Power's good," he murmured.

She smiled and wrapped her arms around his neck. "Yes, it is," she whispered up to him.

"But I don't want to marry you just to get more power," he replied.

Her heart dropped. "You don't?" she asked.

211

He shook his head. "No. I don't," he said softly. "I want to marry you because I can't live without you. I want to marry you because you are the most amazing woman in the world. I want to marry you because I love you with everything that I am."

She exhaled slowly. "Wow. That's good," she breathed, her eyes filling with tears. "That's really good."

He placed a tender kiss on her lips, then met her eyes again. "Two questions," he said.

She nodded, breathless.

"One, do we have to wait until Samhain?" he said with a teasing gleam in his eye. "And two, when do we get to go on our honeymoon?"

She smiled and reached up to kiss him back. "It's only a few days away," she said. "So, yes, unfortunately, we have to wait. And two, as soon as we whip the demon's butt, we're off on our honeymoon."

The teasing left his eyes and took both of her hands in his. "I would do anything to keep you out of this fight with the demon," he said earnestly. "But I know it's your destiny, and you need to be there. But, it's my destiny too, and together we are going to beat it."

She nodded, her throat tight with emotion. "We have to," she said hoarsely. "Because I need to find out if there's just one baby in there or a litter."

He kissed her thoroughly, pulled her close, and sheltered her in his arms. "I love you, Hazel," he said between kisses. "You are my life."

"I love you too," she replied, her body shivering with need. "And I can't wait for the honeymoon."

Chapter Thirty

Henry slipped his arm through Rowan's as they walked toward the Still Room. The afternoon sun was starting its descent, and the air was beginning to get a little cooler. The trees had already begun to turn shades of red, gold, and brown, and flocks of Canada Geese were flying overhead practicing maneuvers.

Henry glanced over at Rowan, seeing her brow furrow as she worked out some problem in her mind. He longed to turn her and kiss her right there on her forehead. He sighed; actually, he longed to carry her away to some safe place where there were no demons, or Samhain, or anything else that would stop them from making slow passionate love all day long.

"Henry?" Rowan asked, wondering why he was staring at her with such an odd expression on his face. "Henry?"

He shook his head, tearing himself away from the fleeting fantasy he'd been experiencing, and smiled at her. "Yes?" he asked.

"What were you thinking about?"

He pondered for only a moment about telling her that he had been picturing them both naked on a beach on some deserted island and decided that distraction was a better option. "I've been thinking about handfasting," he replied, delighted to see the surprise on her face.

"Handfasting?" she stammered.

He smiled. So that was it, that's what she'd been worrying about. He noticed that since Hazel mentioned it at the end of their meeting, Rowan had been more anxious than usual. "Do you realize that the custom came about in the 16th century in Scotland," he continued.

She shook her head. "No. No, I didn't," she replied.

He nodded. "Yes, as a matter of fact…" he paused when she stopped walking, slipped her arm out from beneath his, and folded both of her arms across her chest.

"What?" he asked nervously.

"Did you know that although I'm not nearly as good as Cat when someone has thoughts that exude a lot of emotion, I can read them?" she asked.

He inhaled sharply. "Um, no. No, I didn't realize that," he replied slowly.

The corner of her mouth lifted, and she nodded. "And really, you should have imagined a blanket," she teased. "Sand can be quite, um, abrasive when you're…moving like that."

His jaw dropped. "Rowan," he exclaimed, surprised.

"Oh, and cute butt, professor," she teased.

"Really?" he replied, a wide smile on his face. "And I'm not supposed to respond to that?"

Laughing, she turned and ran away from him towards the Still Room.

"You can run, but you can't hide," he yelled as he ran after her.

He caught her just as she got to the door, grabbed her shoulders, and turned her round to face him. Still laughing, she leaned back against the door, her face alight with mirth.

She was simply too much to resist, Henry thought. He pulled her against him and crushed her lips with his, allowing all his longing and love pour into the emotionally charged kiss.

She gasped softly, and he dove deeper, tasting and teasing, exploring and ravishing. She trembled in his arms and he pulled her even closer, his blood pounding in his head. She sobbed his name and ran her hands over his chest, nearly driving him over the edge.

Taking a deep breath, he lifted his head and looked down on her swollen lips and passion-filled eyes. "Do you know how much I want you?" he whispered, his voice tense with need.

She nodded slowly. "As much as I want you," she murmured.

He put his hand on the doorknob behind her. "What would happen…" he asked.

She shook her head. "I don't know," she replied softly. "I don't know if I care."

He took another deep breath and released the doorknob. He cared. Her safety, the power of the spell, the unity of the sisters. All of that was more important than a night of passion.

He lowered his head, so their foreheads touched. "I love you," he said simply.

"I love you back," she replied.

"Why don't we get married on Samhain?" he suggested.

She giggled nervously, grateful for the way he was letting the passion cool. "That's a great idea," she whispered, lifting her hand and stroking his chin. "And I have an even better one to add to that suggestion."

"What's that?" he asked, lifting her hand to his mouth and kissing it.

"We should have an extra blanket in the car," she whispered. "I know a really secluded beach we can stop at on the way home."

He lifted his head and met her eyes, saw the humor, but also the passion. He shook his head.

"No," he said. "Our first time should be on a feather mattress, with silk sheets and scattered rose petals." He ran his hand up and down her arm. "There should be wax candles and soft music. Someplace I can slowly undress you, savoring every moment."

She trembled and nodded. "Sounds perfect," she sighed. "Suddenly, I'm looking forward to Samhain."

He leaned forward again, his mouth only inches from her own. "I'm looking forward to all the days and nights after it," he whispered before he kissed her again.

Chapter Thirty-one

The next morning, Donovan parked his car in front of his office building, quickly grabbed his briefcase, and hurried out of the vehicle. Joseph had accessed the records at the police station and discovered that it had indeed been filed away before he was notified. The bulletin also had information about the escape that hadn't been released to the general public, but Joseph shared it with Donovan. With the other coven's old leaders on the loose, Donovan realized that he needed to get any vital information out of his office right away. The rest of the coven was still loyal to their leaders, and Ben could easily order one of them to destroy his office and, if they got lucky, him along with it.

He dashed across the sidewalk towards the door and, in his hurry, nearly ran into someone walking down the street. "I'm so sorry," he began, turning to look at the woman he'd pushed to the side. "Are you hurt?"

"No...," she looked up at him. "Donovan?"

"Wanda?" he asked, surprised at the look of despair on her face. "Are you okay?

She nodded quickly, but as she moved to walk around him, he could see tears well up in her eyes. He placed his hand on her arm to stop her. "Want to come upstairs and talk about it?" he asked.

She took a deep breath and impatiently dashed away her tears. "Why would you want to talk to me?" she asked, her tone a mixture of bitterness and grief.

"Because once we were friends," he replied. "Right?"

She nodded. "Before you showed your true colors and chose the Willoughby side," she said, but her words didn't carry the sting they used to.

"I was always on their side," he confessed. "I just thought I could change things by helping the coven see the Willoughbys were right all along. We never had the power to control the demon. It's not a benevolent creature on earth to bless our lives. Its sole purpose is to gain power,

221

and it doesn't care who or what it destroys to reach its goal."

She sighed softly, which infuriated Donovan.

He grabbed both of her upper arms and shook her once. "Don't you see it?" he demanded. "How many people…how many of our friends… has it influenced and destroyed? How many people…who used to be good people…have turned into psychotic killers for this thing?"

She looked up, and he realized the sigh hadn't been sarcastic but heart-felt. "Ben has," she sobbed, her eyes filled with tears once more. "Ben has, and I'm afraid he's going to pull my father in with him."

Donavon glanced around them to see who might have overheard, but the sidewalk was empty. "We need to talk, in private," he said, his voice low.

He guided her into the building and then to the elevator bank.

"I shouldn't be…" she began but stopped when he met her eyes and shook his head, signaling for her to stop.

"Not here," he whispered.

222

He led her from the elevator down the hall to his office and closed the door.

"I wanted…" she began again, and he shook his head once more.

He walked over to a small stereo on his credenza and turned on a rock and roll station, then he adjusted the volume, so it was fairly loud. Only then did he lead her over to his desk and offer her a chair.

"Now we can talk," he said, sitting next to her at the desk. "I discovered a while back that my office had been bugged. I'm not sure if it still is, but I don't want to take any chances."

She nervously looked around the room and then stood up. "I shouldn't be here," she said, "I should not be talking to you. If anyone found out…"

He nodded. "You're right," he said. "If anyone found out, you could be in jeopardy. But tell me, how safe do you feel right now, in the situation you're in?"

She stood still for a long moment and slowly shook her head. "I'm not safe," she said, slipping back down into the chair. "I know I'm not safe."

"You know that Ben and the rest of them escaped?" Donovan asked.

She nodded.

"How do you know that the demon is influencing Ben?" he asked.

"The guard they killed," she said. "Ben did it."

"You know they killed a guard during the escape?"

A single tear slipped down her cheek, and she nodded again. "Yes," she whispered.

"Only Joseph knew that," Donovan said. "That information was not released to the public. So, how did you know?"

She placed her hands over her face and sobbed. "He didn't have to kill him," she cried. "He was going home for the day. He wasn't going to do anything to them. Ben just did it for spite."

"You were there?" Donovan asked.

"I helped them escape," she said.

"And you know where they are?"

She nodded. "But you can't go there," she said. "He'll kill my father. He'll kill you. Hell, he'll kill me. He's gotten stronger."

"Do you have a place you can go?" Donovan asked. "Somewhere, out of town, where he can't find you?"

She paused for a moment, searching her mind for options. "I have a friend, from college," she said. "She lives in Iowa, Quad Cities. She's always inviting me to visit her."

"Is she of the blood?"

She shook her head. "No, she's just mortal. Why should that matter?"

"Because at this point, those of the blood are divided, and we don't know who we can trust," he replied. "So, you're safer being with someone who has no idea of what's going on."

Wanda thought about how nice it would be to get away, far away from the danger. Then she thought about her father, who was still connected to Ben.

"I should stay here," she said. "My father." She met Donovan's eyes. "He isn't bad, he isn't into power trips, he's just weak, and he lets people with stronger personalities lead him. I don't think he wants to be in the situation he's in."

"I'll help him," Donovan promised. "But you need to leave. You need to let me know where they're hiding out, and you need to leave."

"I'm so confused," she said. "I really want to leave, I'm so tired of all of this. But…"

"Wanda, for your safety, you need to go."

Chapter Thirty-two

Donovan, his phone to his ear, watched from his office window as Wanda walked to her car. He prayed that she would take his advice and get out of town, but in the meantime, he needed to be sure he did everything he could to stop Ben and his cronies.

"Joseph," he said when the phone was answered. "I need to talk to you right away. Can you come to my office?"

He paused and nodded. "Okay, yeah, twenty minutes would be great."

Hanging up, he turned back to his desk. For the next few days, he would be spending nearly every waking hour at the Willoughbys farm, so he needed to pack up anything he might need during that time.

Slipping off his suit jacket and hanging it on the back of his chair, he then sat in his chair and pulled a memory stick from his desk drawer. Turning on his computer, he accessed the cases he'd been working on and downloaded them to the memory stick and then uploaded them to the company's cloud system. He pulled hard copies of certain documents from their files and set them aside so he could put them in his briefcase.

Then he clicked on his mailbox folder and waited for his emails to download. He leaned back in his chair and waited, impatiently tapping his fingers against the desk. As soon as he scanned his emails, he could pack everything up. He looked at his watch, Joseph should be arriving at any moment.

A ringing sound notified him that all of his emails had downloaded, and he sat up and began to go through them. The first few were staff memorandums that he quickly read and filed. Several were messages from clients with information he'd requested. He reviewed the information and then forwarded them to his personal email account that he could easily access. There were two emails about community events that some of the civic organizations he belonged to were sponsoring. Most of them were spam emails that he could easily delete without even having to open them. Finally, there was one addressed to him that didn't look like spam but was from an email address that he didn't recognize. He clicked on the message to open it and found a voice memo.

He moved his mouse, so it pointed to the file, but hesitated a moment before he clicked on it. For some reason, his heart was pounding, and his hands were clammy with sweat. He looked away from his computer and took a deep breath to calm his nerves.

"What the hell is wrong with you, Farrington?" he asked himself. "Something is not going to jump out at you from a voice message."

Slightly disgusted at himself, he turned back to the computer and clicked on the file.

"Hello, Donovan. It's been a little while, hasn't it?"

The voice of the demon filled the room. Urgently, Donovan clicked on the file to close it, but it wouldn't close.

"I'm afraid once you've opened the file, you can't turn back, my boy."

He tried closing the email application, but nothing on his computer was responding.

"Do you miss me? Do you miss the power I gave you?"

Frantically, Donovan pushed the button to turn off the computer, but it did nothing, the message continued.

"I miss you, Donovan. I miss the talks we used to have. The punishments I would eke out when you didn't obey me. You do remember those punishments, don't you, Donovan?"

Suddenly, the scars on Donovan's back began to burn. He clenched his teeth as the pain increased, and the burning intensified.

"Stop it," Donovan moaned. "Stop it."

He struggled out of his chair, holding on to the desk as he made his way to the computer's power cord.

"I can't stop, Donovan. And more to the point, you can't stop me."

Sharp pain brought him to his knees. It was if the demon was in the room, beating him again. He felt the scars reopen, felt blood ooze from the wounds, felt the burn as if his back was on fire.

Crawling forward, he reached out, grabbed hold of the power cord, and pulled it out of the electrical socket.

"Oh, sorry, Donovan, that didn't seem to work either, did it? You need to understand, I am back."

His office door burst open; Joseph ran inside and saw Donovan on the floor.

"The computer," Donovan moaned. "Kill the computer."

"I am more powerful, and I am going to kill you and the…"

With one powerful stroke of his arm, Joseph knocked the computer off the desk and smashed it into the wall. The office was suddenly silent.

Joseph bent down next to Donovan. "Okay, this was not what I was expecting when I got your call," he said. "Can you stand up?"

Donovan nodded. "Yeah, I think so," he said, wincing as he moved.

Joseph stood and offered Donovan his hand, helping him to his feet. "Turn around," Joseph ordered.

"I'm fine," Donovan replied.

"Turn around. Cut the crap," Joseph said.

Donovan slowly turned, and Joseph grimaced when he saw the blood stains on the back of Donovan's shirt. Blood and sweat had plastered the cotton material to his back and the welts and scars were clearly visible.

"Hope this wasn't your favorite shirt," Joseph quipped.

Donovan chuckled. "How's it look?"

"Like crap," Joseph replied, then he paused. "You mean your back or the shirt?"

"My back," Donovan answered.

"It looks like crap, too," Joseph answered. "But it's nothing Rowan and Henry can't take care of."

"Yeah, not Rowan," Donovan said, turning around. "Call Henry and ask him to come down here and meet us. I don't want the Willoughbys to know. Not yet."

Chapter Thirty-three

Cat, Rowan, and Hazel were in Henry's apartment above the barn that Hazel had created at the beginning of the summer when he'd first arrived.

With her hands on her hips, Hazel slowly turned around, critiquing the area. "I don't know," she said. "I think I could add another loft with two bedrooms over there without much trouble. And it will cover up some of these floor-to-ceiling windows, so we don't have any more shooters aiming at us from the road."

"Okay, that will work for Joseph and Donovan," Rowan said. "But how about Seamus, Dustin, and Finias?"

Hazel sighed. "Well, how about if I put them on the third-floor in-law apartment of the house," she suggested.

"We don't have a third-floor in-law apartment," Cat replied.

Hazel grinned. "We don't yet," she said.

234

Cat walked to the window and looked across to the house. "You know, if you added some dormers, that could be really cute," she said.

Hazel nodded. "And really, with the unfinished attic already up there," she assured her sisters. "I could have it done in no time."

Cat started to laugh, then stopped suddenly, her eyes widening in fear.

"What's wrong?" Rowan asked immediately.

"Something's happening to Donovan," Cat said, her voice filled with terror. "He's hurt. I can feel that he's hurt."

"Joseph went to see him at his office about fifteen minutes ago," Hazel said. "He should be there any moment now." She turned to Rowan. "Call Joseph and tell him to hurry."

"On it!" Rowan replied, picking up her phone.

Hazel turned back to Cat. "Can you picture him?" she asked. "Is he still in his office?"

Cat closed her eyes and concentrated for a moment, trying to push the fear and anxiety away so she could clear her mind. She took a deep breath and then saw him lying on the floor, next to his desk.

"He's in his office," she said. "But he's lying on the floor."

"Is he alone?" Hazel asked. "Or is Joseph walking into an ambush?"

Cat concentrated again. "He's alone, but he's in pain," she replied. "I need to go, right now."

"Okay, I'll send you," Hazel asked.

"What do you mean?" Cat exclaimed.

"Really? I can move building materials, but you don't think I can send you to Donovan's office," Hazel answered.

"Oh. Really? You can do that?" Cat asked, then she nodded at Hazel. "I'm ready. Yes, send me!"

"Joseph should be at his office," Rowan said. "Are you sure you don't want to wait?"

Cat shook her head. "No, I can't wait," she replied. "I need to be there."

"Okay, you need to work with me on this," Hazel said. "You need to clear your mind again, okay?"

Cat nodded.

"You really need to focus on where you want to be," Hazel replied. "But try to keep the fear at a minimum. Positive thoughts help with travel."

Cat shook her head. "Positive thoughts?" she asked.

Hazel put her hands on her sister's shoulders. "Just think about how much you love him," she suggested. "Push the worry to the side."

Cat exhaled slowly and smiled. "Thank you," she said, then she took a deep breath and closed her eyes. "Okay, I'm ready."

"Now tap your heels three times," Hazel began.

Cat opened one eye. "What in the world..."

Hazel laughed, waved her arms, and Cat disappeared.

"Why did you do that?" Rowan asked.

"If she's pissed at me, she won't be worried about Donovan," Hazel said. "By the time she remembers to be worried, she'll already be in his office."

Chapter Thirty-four

"The Willoughbys already know something's up," Joseph told Donovan. "I got a call from Rowan to run to your office. Cat felt something."

"How could she…" Donovan began.

"What happened to you?" Cat exclaimed as she suddenly appeared in Donovan's office.

"How did you get here?" he insisted, turning so she couldn't see his back.

"Do you really think if Hazel can move building materials, she can't move a person?" she answered, repeating Hazel's own words to her just moments ago. "I felt something was wrong. I felt like you were in pain, so I came."

"I'm fine," Donovan insisted.

"You were lying on the floor," Cat argued. "I saw you."

"I dropped something," Donovan countered. "No big deal."

Cat looked past Donovan to the mirror over the credenza and saw the reflection of the back of his shirt. She gasped, and her eyes filled with tears. Donovan looked over his shoulder, saw the mirror, and realized what she'd seen.

"Who did this to you?" she asked.

"I'm not in league with him," Donovan replied defensively. "I didn't do what he wanted. I haven't betrayed you or your family."

Cat stepped forward and gently placed her hand on his cheek. "I know that," she said simply.

Like all the air had been taken out of his sails, Donovan slumped back and sat on the edge of his desk, wincing slightly at his wounds. "You know?" he asked, confused.

"Of course, I know," she replied. "You are a good and honorable man. You only associated with the demon because you thought it would help."

Donovan breathed a long sigh of relief. "I'm sorry," he said. "I should have trusted you more. I didn't think you would believe me."

"I'm a little confused here," Joseph said. "You called me about twenty minutes ago, asking me to come down to your office. Did you know the demon was going to attack you?"

Shaking his head, Donovan reached onto his desk for the notepad he used to write down the information from Wanda. "No. That's not why I called you," he replied. "I had Wanda Wildes in my office…"

"You had Wanda in your office?" Cat asked. "Alone? You and Wanda?"

"Getting back to Donovan being a good and honorable man," Joseph inserted with a smile.

Cat turned and glared at Joseph. "Man being the operative word," she replied, then she took a deep breath and released it. "Fine. Why was Wanda up here? In your office? With the door closed?"

"Because she was frightened," Donovan said.

241

Cat rolled her eyes. "Oh, give me a break," she said. "The frightened victim looking for a little solace."

"She told me that she helped her father and the rest of the men escape," Donovan continued.

"She did what?" Cat exclaimed. "She could go to jail for admitting that."

Donovan nodded and then looked over at Joseph. "This is a little late," he said. "But this is off the record, client-attorney privilege."

Joseph crossed his arms over his chest and nodded, unsmiling, at Donovan. "You're right, it is a little late," he replied. "But go ahead."

"She said that Ben Stoughton frightens her," he continued. "She said that he's lost whatever compassion or common sense he had. She said that he murdered the guard in the parking lot."

"Seems like the demon feeds on stuff like that, murder and mayhem. And now, these guys escape, and suddenly the demon comes calling with renewed power," Joseph said. "There's got to be a connection."

"Right. And we don't know how much power he's given to Ben," Donovan said. "I've got an address, but sending regular uniforms into a situation like this could be suicide."

Joseph nodded. "And I still don't know how many of my men are actually his," he admitted. "He was chief for a long time."

"So, someone could be coming for us right now," Cat inserted. "We need to get back home. The rest need to know that we're not just protecting ourselves against Ben and his crew, now we need to be on guard against the demon."

"You drive Donovan's car," Joseph said. "And I'll follow you in mine."

Donovan stood up, pain shooting down his back as he did, and walked across the room to his destroyed computer.

"That's not going to help you," Cat said, looking at the scattered pile of plastic and wires.

Donovan bent over and pulled the memory stick from the damaged case. "No, but this will," he said, picking up his files and putting them in his briefcase. "Okay, let's go."

Chapter Thirty-five

Cat pulled Donovan's car close to the back porch and put it in park. She turned to Donovan, whose face was pallid and strained. "How are you doing?" she asked.

He nodded slowly. "I'm okay," he breathed. "It's taken a little more out of me than I thought it would."

"I'll come around and help you out," she told him. "Stay right there."

Joseph pulled up behind them and hurried out of his vehicle, meeting Cat at Donovan's door. "How's he doing?" he asked before she opened the door.

She shook her head. "Not good," she said. "I think there's more to this than just reopening old wounds."

She opened the door and started the help him out.

"Hold on there," Seamus called from the back porch. "Leave him be for a moment."

Cat eased Donovan back into his seat and looked over at Seamus. "What's going on?"

Jogging quickly down the stairs, Seamus hurried over to the passenger door. He leaned in to look at Donovan. "Before you come in, may I have a look at your back, boyo?" he asked.

"Sure," Donovan replied, leaning forward in the seat. "But why?"

Seamus reached out, lightly laid his hand on Donovan's back, and quickly pulled it back. "It's as I thought," he said. "We won't want to be bringing you into the house."

"What?" Cat asked. "Why not?"

Seamus looked over his shoulder at her. "If you'd just step back a little ways, darling," he said, then he closed the car door with Donovan still inside. "We don't want to spread the infection."

"Infection?" Cat asked. "What infection?"

"Joseph called Henry and told him what happened," Seamus explained. "And described how Donovan was feeling. Open wounds don't cause that kind of pain. But wounds that have been infected would."

246

"Infected with what?" Cat asked.

Seamus nodded and smiled at her. "And that, darling, is what I need to discover," he said, then he turned to Rowan and Henry, who were standing nearby. "I need you to test both Cat and Joseph and see if they've been infected."

"There's an isolation area in the Still Room," Rowan said. "Let's head down there."

"How can I be infected?" Cat asked.

"Where you within a few feet of Donovan?" Seamus asked.

She nodded.

"Well, until I know exactly what he's infected with, I don't know how far it can travel or how it's transmitted," he replied. "And I'd rather not allow it to infect the rest of us."

Cat and Joseph followed Rowan and Henry to the Still Room. Then Seamus looked up to see Hazel standing on the porch. "Hazel, why don't you go back inside," he suggested. "I'd like you and the baby as far away from

247

this as possible. Dustin, could you put the car, Donovan, and me in some kind of big plastic bag, so we don't infect anyone else?"

"Wait," Finias called, jogging down the steps and joining Seamus. "I'm a healer too. I can help."

"Good," Seamus said. "I gather I'll need all the help I can get." He looked back at Dustin. "Now, please."

Suddenly, the area was covered in a bio-containment tent with a filtered air converter at one end.

"Nice job," Seamus said, looking around. "Leave it to an engineer to get it right."

Just then, two bio-hazards suits appeared on the ground next to them and Seamus chuckled. "Suit up, my friend," he said to Finias. "We've got some work to do."

Once both men were suited up, Seamus opened the door again and helped Donovan out. "Are you strong enough to stand, or would you like a chair?" he asked.

Surprised at how weak he was, Donovan faltered as his knees nearly gave out underneath him.

"A chair it is," Seamus said. "Dustin, a few more items, please. A tall chair for this young man to sit upon, perhaps some surgical tools, along with a vacuum trap geared for biohazardous waste."

A moment later, a tall metal stool with a short back stood next to them, along with a laboratory table equipped with a vacuum line attached to a trap flask, as well as a pouch of surgical tools.

"This'll do nicely," Seamus said, guiding Donovan to the chair.

He picked up the scissors and cut away the back of Donovan's shirt. Donovan winced when he peeled back the cotton, exposing the raw flesh. "Your back was fine this morning?" Seamus asked Donovan over his shoulder.

Donovan nodded. "The scars were completely healed, and almost gone," he replied. "Rowan gave me some Calendula ointment that was working wonders."

"You had no fever or pain?" Seamus asked.

Donovan shook his head. "No, none at all," he replied.

249

Seamus moved slightly to the side. "Finias, grab hold of the vacuum line and stand here, next to me," he said. "I want to see something."

Finias brought the line with the narrow vacuum head over and was able to see Donovan's back for the first time. The wounds were red and raw, but there were also pockets of pus alongside the wounds.

"This looks worse than it did when we first helped him," Finias said.

"No infection?" Seamus asked.

"None," Finias replied. "Only wounds."

"I thought as much," Seamus replied. "Now hold that line right underneath the scalpel."

"Scalpel?" Donovan asked, concerned.

"Aye, but I'll be gentle, lad, I promise."

Seamus pressed the scalpel to the bottom of one of the pockets and gently applied pressure. The sharp blade cut through the damaged flesh, and suddenly pus began to seep out around the knife. "Now Finias," Seamus demanded. "Bring the vacuum here and suction up all the pus."

Clamping the nozzle over the puncture, they both watched in amazement as the yellow pus traveled down the plastic tubing, changing to black as it traveled toward the trap flask.

"What the hell is that?" Finias asked.

"Well, if I'm not mistaken, if we were to take a slide and put it under a microscope, we'd find an amoeba of sorts," Seamus said. "A dark and putrid creature. Nothing like medical science has ever seen, but it's been used since time immemorial to seep into the hearts and minds of men."

Seamus turned and saw Dustin standing just on the other side of the plastic wall. "Good man," he said to Dustin. "Is there a way you can change the fluid in the flask to holy water?"

Dustin smiled slowly and nodded. "And perhaps I ought to put an extra coating around the flask to make it indestructible."

251

Seamus laughed. "Aye, good idea."

Suddenly, high-pitched screams of destruction echoed through the containment room. Seamus nodded. "That did the trick," he said. "And now, let's move on to the next blister."

Thirty minutes later, all of the blisters had been drained, and the high-pitched squealing coming from the flask had stopped. Seamus stepped back, exhausted, and nodded. "I think we got them all," he said. "But just in case, we need to cleanse your back." He leaned forward over Donovan's shoulder. "It's going to sting."

Donovan nodded, feeling stronger now that the infection was removed. "I'm okay," he said. "Go for it."

Seamus turned to Dustin. "A spray bottle filled with holy water and also a container of Rowan's calendula ointment, please."

A minute later, both appeared on the table. "Handy that," Seamus said, picking up the spray bottle and pointing it at Donovan's back. "If we've done our job right, the sting should be minimal. But I don't want to miss one of those little buggers that might have burrowed down into your skin."

He sprayed the water liberally over Donovan's back, and there were some areas that stung like salt had just been sprayed into his wounds, but after a minute or two of pain, the stinging stopped and Donovan felt his strength returning. Finally, Seamus applied the ointment. Donovan felt its healing properties work immediately. He stood up, his legs strong underneath him, and turned to Seamus and Finias. "Thank you for all you just did," he said. "But what happened to me?"

"Let's get out of this containment room, and I'll explain to the whole family," he said. He studied Donovan for a moment and then asked. "Are you strong enough to transport yourself."

Donovan took a quick inventory of how he felt and nodded. "Yes. Why?"

"You need to change out of those clothes and then burn them," Seamus replied. "Just in case we missed anything." Then he looked around through the clear plastic of the containment room and smiled. "And I'm thinking you'd like a little more privacy that this."

Donovan chuckled and nodded. "I agree," he said.

He looked out through the plastic and saw Rowan standing close by. "Can I use the isolation area in the Still Room?" he asked.

She nodded. "After you're done, just step out of the room and press the decontamination button next to the door," she replied. "I'll make sure holy water is added to the process."

He nodded. "Thanks," he said, and then he disappeared.

Chapter Thirty-six

"I suppose we now understand a little more about turning the hearts of the children to their parents," Agnes said, as the family sat around the dining room table. She turned to Seamus, who was sitting next to Rowan. "Seamus, your quick action saved us all from being infected. Thank you."

"Yes," Donovan said. "I agree. How did you even think to check for infection?"

"Well now," Seamus replied. "In my profession, I've had the privilege of participating in a few archeological digs around the world and, of course, I've read of others. And when you begin to deal with the unknown, from tombs to hidden cities, you have to always assume that something malevolent is waiting for you on the other side. I've had colleagues die because they were infected with an ancient virus that they released when they opened up an old tomb."

"That sounds fairly pessimistic," Rowan replied. "Always expect the worst."

Seamus turned to her and smiled. "No, my darling, don't expect the worst," he said. "Expect the amazing. But protect yourself from the worst, and then you'll be able to enjoy the amazing."

Rowan leaned over and kissed his cheek. "I like that explanation much better," she replied. "And so, what do we need to protect ourselves from now?"

"We have to assume the demon is stronger," Henry said. "The fact that he could not only communicate with Donovan but infect him means that somehow he's gained some strength."

"And I'd link it directly to Ben, Wade, Neal, and Buck," Donovan said. "They've done something that's given the demon strength."

"But we don't even know where they are," Hazel said.

"Yes, we do," Joseph said, sending her an apologetic look. "That's why Donovan called me to his office in the first place. They are hiding out in a cabin near Kettle Moraine."

"What?" Agnes asked. She turned to Donovan. "I know we suspected, but how did you find that out?"

"I literally ran into Wanda in front of my office," Donovan replied. "I could tell she was upset, and I invited her to come upstairs. She's frightened. She said that Ben's personality has gotten even worse."

"How could it get worse than it is?" Agnes remarked. "What did he do?"

"A guard was killed during the escape," Donovan said. "Wanda said that his death was totally unnecessary, but Ben did it because he enjoyed having the power."

Agnes nodded. "That sounds like Ben," she agreed, then she stopped and shook her head. "No, actually, it doesn't sound like him. In the past few years, he's been much more strategic, less impulsive. He wanted his coven to have more power, but he wouldn't do anything to jeopardize its standing."

"Now, it sounds like it's all about power with no strategy or common sense," Donovan said.

"So, he's being influenced by the demon," Finias said. "The demon doesn't care about those who serve him, he's only concerned with his needs."

"Which tells me that it's even more important for all of us to stay together," Joseph said. "Because we are the only thing standing in the way of the demon."

"Right," Hazel said. "There are extra rooms in the apartment over the barn. I thought that Donovan and Joseph could stay there with Henry."

"Works for me," Henry said.

"And then I thought we'd put Finias, Seamus, and Dustin in the in-law-suite in the attic," she continued.

Agnes looked confused. "What in-law suite in the attic?" she asked.

Hazel grinned. "Well, once this meeting is done and I can get some time up there with Cat and Rowan, there will be an in-law suite in the attic."

"Would you like a little help?" Dustin asked.

Hazel shook her head. "Thanks, Dad, but Rowan, Cat, and I already have a plan in mind," she said. "And I think we'd like to surprise all of you."

Finias nodded. "Okay, well, then we can drive into town and get our things," he said.

"Seriously?" Dustin asked him. "Just tell me what you want, and I'll bring it here. And then we can use the time to decide how we can best protect ourselves."

Chapter Thirty-seven

Cat, Rowan, and Hazel climbed up the creaky wooden stairs to the attic. Taking the lead, Cat brushed away the cobwebs hanging from the ceiling. "How long has it been since we were up here?" she asked.

"I think the last time was the famous bat incident," Hazel reminded her.

"Oh, when that bat swooped over us and nearly got caught in Cat's hair," Rowan said, frantically searching the space for any signs of an errant bat.

"It didn't nearly get caught in her hair," Hazel corrected her. "Bats have internal radar, they might have gotten close, but they wouldn't have landed on her head."

"It was close enough for me," Cat replied. "I never wanted to have anything to do with the attic after that."

Once they stepped onto the wooden attic floor, they looked around. "This is actually pretty cool," Hazel said, slowly walking down the center of the space. "The ceiling is easily twelve feet, so we won't have to raise the roof."

"Spoken as an expert at raising the roof," Rowan teased.

Hazel turned and grinned. "If you've got…" she replied. Then she turned back to the task at hand. "So, since the plumbing is already at the back of the house, let's put the bathroom and the mini-kitchen back here."

"They're going to have a mini-kitchen?" Cat asked.

"Why not," Hazel replied. "The kitchen is three stories down. That's quite a ways for a snack."

Cat nodded. "Okay, that's a good point."

Hazel turned to the side. "I think we could put a little sitting area over here," she said, walking across the width of the space. She stopped when she came to a wooden wall with a door. "Hey, what's in here?"

Cat shrugged. "As I recall, it was the 'don't touch that stuff' area," she said.

"Really?" Hazel replied, excited. "Well, let's check it out then."

With a wave of her hand, she unlocked the door, and it flung open wide. She hesitantly poked her head into the opening. "Are there any bats in here?" she called out, reaching over and pulling a string that turned on a bare bulb light.

"Wow!" she exclaimed, entering the small room. "No bats, but possibilities."

Cat and Rowan quickly followed behind her.

The room size was about ten by ten, and it was filled with old furniture, cedar chests, an ancient rocking chair, and several stacks of boxes. Cat walked over to the largest cedar chest that was ornately carved with symbols of the seasons. She gently ran her hand over it, clearing away years of dust and exposing a golden stain.

"Open it," Rowan encouraged.

Bending down, she turned the metal lock, so she could lift the latch over it. Then she pushed the top of the chest up to reveal a layer of sheeting.

262

"White sheets?" Hazel asked, peering over Cat's shoulder. "Wow, that's exciting. I think we have enough bedding."

Rowan shook her head. "No, in the old days, they used sheeting to protect other things," she explained as she moved around her sisters and carefully lifted the sheet away. Then she picked up several small square packets. "And these are linen packets with lavender inside. They keep away moths."

"So, what's in there that they were protecting?" Hazel asked.

Rowan removed one more layer of sheeting, then picked up an old dress box. She carefully removed the lid from the box and gasped softly as she lifted a beautiful flowing white gown in soft, silk georgette. "Look at this," she said with awe. "It's so beautiful."

The dress had a scooped neck, an empire waistline and draped in soft tiers to the floor. "It's gorgeous," Hazel said, running her hand over the delicate material.

"You should try it on," Rowan said to Hazel.

263

Hazel stepped back and shook her head. "No, you found it," she said, trying to keep the regret from her voice. "You should try it on."

Rowan snorted softly. "Did you see how long this dress was?" she asked her much taller sister. "I would look like a little girl trying to wear my mother's wedding dress. Not a good look."

"Really?" Hazel asked, making sure her sister really meant it.

"Really," Rowan replied.

Hazel quickly stripped down to her underwear. Rowan and Cat held the dress over her head, and she slipped into it. The cool fabric slid sensuously over her body and fit as if it were made for her. She stepped back and slowly turned around. "Well, what do you think?" she asked.

Cat brushed a tear from her eye as she looked at her little sister. "You look so beautiful," she said. "You have to wear this on Samhain."

Rowan, her eyes filled with tears, nodded. "It's so perfect," she whispered, her voice tight with emotion. "Joseph is going to fall in love all over again." Then Rowan glanced around the room and found what she was looking for. "I thought I saw it when we entered the room."

With a wave of her hand, a dust cover was lifted into the air and tossed on the ground. An old, full-length mirror had been underneath it. Hazel stepped across the room and stood in front of it, her face reflecting her amazement. "It's perfect," she said softly. "Just totally perfect."

Then she turned to her sisters. "Are you sure?" she asked. "You found it."

"It's your dress," Rowan said. "It doesn't matter who found it."

Cat turned back to the trunk and pulled out the next dress box and saw that there was a third underneath it. "Do you think?" she asked, setting the box down and then pulling out the other one. "They saw us? They saw our day?"

Rowan came over and took the box from Cat's hands. "There's only one way to find out."

She took her box over to a small table a few feet away and carefully opened it. Inside was an ivory batiste gown with delicate lace around the neckline, sleeves, and hem. In just a few moments, Cat and Hazel were helping her try it on. The tiny buttons all the way up the back took a little while to fasten, but finally she could turn and look into the mirror.

The fitted sleeves and natural waist emphasized her petite frame. The skirt was full, but without a tulle petticoat underneath, it fell in soft folds to the floor. The ivory color complemented her red-headed complexion and the old-fashioned, romantic look of the dress matched her personality.

"You look like a princess," Hazel said.

Rowan turned to one side and then the other as she stared at herself in the mirror. "It's made to order," she said in amazement. "It's just perfect." Then she turned to Cat. "Okay, it's your turn."

With trembling hands, Cat lifted the top from her box. The white cotton voile dress had dropped shoulders with ruffles across the bodice and down the sleeves, and a white embroidered paneled corset fit around the waist. The skirt was full and flowing with yards of the light cotton fabric.

"Try it on!" Hazel said. "Quickly!"

With the help of her sisters, Cat slipped into the dress that reminded her of her Jamaican heritage. She tightened the corset and turned to look.

"You look like an island queen," Rowan said. "It's so perfect for you, Cat."

Cat stood, transfixed, staring at herself in the mirror. "It's like every dress I've ever imagined all rolled up into one," she said. "This is so perfect." Then her eyes widened in dismay. "But what about Mom?"

Rowan smiled. "Mom can wear that same dress she wore when she married Finias the first time," she said.

"I don't think any other dress would be as romantic as that one."

Cat nodded. "You're right," she said, then she twirled around in front of the mirror. "Suddenly, I can't wait until Samhain."

Hazel and Rowan joined their sister in the mirror, three sisters, different in many ways, yet so similar in others. "This is going to be awesome," Rowan said.

"Yes, it is," Cat replied.

"We're going to knock their socks off," Hazel added, then she looked around the room. "But first, we need to create the in-law suite, or our dads are not going to have any place to sleep tonight."

Chapter Thirty-eight

Dustin slowly walked around the newly created in-law suite, examining the structure and paying close attention to where the rafters and joists connected to the newly constructed knee wall. He shook his head and let out a slow whistle. "That little gal of mine is impressive, to say the least," he said. "The miter cuts couldn't be more perfect."

"Aye," Seamus agreed, looking up into the night sky through the skylights they'd put in. "And for a room with such a small area, she was able to make it feel like we have plenty of space."

Finias walked over to one of the floor-to-ceiling graduated windows that were installed in each dormer. "And she also gave us the ability to have a bird's eye view of the entire area," he remarked. "Which is crucial, considering our situation."

Dustin sighed. "And now it's time to stop talking like a proud father and get down to brass tacks, right?" he

269

asked, walking away from the wall he was examining and back to the common area in the center of the attic.

"I'm afraid so," Finias replied. He gazed around the farmyard once more, noting the lights on in the apartment above the barn, and then turned and joined the other two fathers. He sat down and looked at both men. "I can't trust my visions completely, but I have seen myself more than once walking through a graveyard."

Dustin nodded. "As have I," he replied. "I'm in the family cemetery, and I'm walking past the graves of all those who have gone before me."

"Have you seen your own names of headstones?" Seamus asked with a sigh. "Because it's either my grave or the grave of my great-great-grandfather. I'm truly hoping it's him and not me."

"I haven't seen my name on a headstone," Finias replied. "But the words are too fuzzy to read."

"Which makes sense, considering it's your own vision," Dustin said. "We're not allowed to get too much information about ourselves."

"It must be the Irish luck that let me see my own," Seamus said with a sad grin. "But there's naught we can do about it. We need to move forward to help our daughters, whatever the cost."

"Something Agnes said tonight that didn't totally ring true to me," Dustin said. "Although I thought your handling of Donovan's situation was remarkable, I didn't see it as an example of turning the hearts of the children to their fathers, did you?"

Seamus shook his head. "No, although I consider all of the girls, and, for that matter, both of you, as family now," he replied. "I don't think Donovan qualifies as one of my children. I suppose Henry would be the closest of that group. So, I agree. I think I was just in the right place at the right time."

"So, do you still think there's more we need to do with our daughters?" Finias asked. "Something else that would create a stronger bond for when we fight the demon?"

Dustin shrugged. "Well, it could be as simple as participating in the handfasting with them," he said. "Creating the link between the past and the future. There is a powerful bond created during a handfasting."

"So, if we perform the ceremonies for our daughters, we are creating a more powerful link?" Seamus asked, then he looked at Finias. "And if we are participating in the ceremony, even better."

Finias looked away and shook his head. "There is something I need to speak to both of you about," he said. "I'm not quite sure how to say it."

Seamus shook his head and smiled. "I've seen the way Agnes looks at you," he said. "You were her first love. I think she loved us, Dustin and I, in her own way. But it was never like what you had. All teasing aside, I'm truly hoping that you and she are going to be part of the ceremony as well."

"You don't mind?" Finias asked.

"Well, aye, it's ripping my heart out," Seamus replied with a chuckle. "But I'm not blind man, I know who she favors. How about you, Dustin?"

"I'll always love Agnes, and treasure the time we had together," he said. "And I'll always be grateful that I was able to be a small part of Hazel's life. But I agree with Seamus, Agnes was always your soulmate."

Finias exhaled slowly and nodded. "Thank you," he said. "I'm grateful we have been thrown together like this, grateful that you are both part of my family."

"I feel the same way," Dustin said. "If I'm to go down fighting, I couldn't have picked two finer men to fight alongside."

Seamus sighed. "It's odd, isn't it?" he asked. "Potentially, we have both weddings and funerals to prepare for." He lifted his mug of tea. "Here's to the funeral being in honor of the demon."

Finias and Dustin both lifted their mugs too.

"And long may he rest," Dustin said.

"And long may we live," Finias added.

273

Chapter Thirty-nine

"Mom! Mom! Help me!"

Agnes sat up in her bed, her heart pounding and frantically looked around.

"Hazel?" she asked. "Cat? Rowan?"

"Mom, I'm out here," the voice cried.

Agnes quickly slipped out of bed, grabbed her robe, and put it on as she raced out of her bedroom and into the great room. "Girls?" she called. "Where are you?"

"Mom, please, I'm out here."

She quickly ran to the front door, pulled it open, and stepped out onto the porch. "Where? Where are you? I can't see you?" she called desperately.

"Here, Mom! Here!"

The voice came from the woods, just beyond the property line. Barefoot, Agnes dashed down the stairs and across the front lawn towards the woods. "I'm coming," Agnes called. "I'll be there in a moment."

"Hurry, Mom. Hurry!"

Agnes jogged across the wide expanse of lawn, toward the dark woods. She knew that the protections she'd placed ended at the property line and wondered why any of the girls would risk themselves by going beyond the boundary. "I'm coming," she called again.

Ben Stoughton stood behind a large oak tree, near the edge of the Willoughby property. He held his knife low, so the sharp blade did not glimmer in the light of the moon. All he had to do now was wait, and Agnes would be in his control. He glanced at the rope at his feet, waved his hand, and the rope was suddenly animated and floating in the air. Once she stepped over the property line, the rope would go flying and she'd be pinned to a tree before she even realized what happened to her. He had a gag stuffed in his back pocket, ready to shove it into her mouth before she could scream. And then...he smiled to himself. And then he could decide just how long he wanted to keep her alive.

He peered around the tree again. She was getting closer.

His mind raced back to that day underneath the bleachers. She had gotten away once; she was not going to get away again. This time he was going to take what he wanted. He wanted to see the look on her face when she realized that he was all powerful. The fear on her face when he raped her. Then, the final horror when he was done with her and slowly took her life.

He wished he could stay to witness her family discovering her body in the morning. But he would have to be content with the knowledge that he would have single-handedly destroyed the Willoughby's ability to conquer the demon.

He moved the knife from one hand to the other, wiping the free one on the tree trunk next to him to remove the sweat that had accumulated while he plotted her demise. He licked his lips, and his breathing quickened as she neared. Just a few more yards. He could already imagine the sound her nightgown would make when he tore it from her body. The feel of the soft fabric in his hands as it yielded to his strength.

He rubbed his hand across his upper lip to wipe away the moisture that had formed there. Just a few more feet.

He took a deep breath, ready to send the rope flying noiselessly through the air.

Just a few more steps.

A hand clamped down on Agnes' shoulder, and she gasped.

"What are you doing?" Finias asked.

"One of the girls called out," she said, trying to escape his hold. "Someone's in trouble, I need to go."

Finias pulled her away from the boundary and shook his head. "No. Something's not right," he said.

"Finias, they need me," she exclaimed. "I need to go."

He held her tightly. "Agnes, wait," he said. "Just give me a moment." He waved his hand, and suddenly the forest was filled with light. They both heard a rustling in the woods nearby and then everything was silent.

"Girls?" Agnes called into the woods. "Are you there?"

She turned to him. "They're gone," she cried hysterically. "You let someone take them. Why didn't you let me go to them?"

"Agnes, close your eyes and picture your daughters," he said, holding firmly to her upper arms. "Find them in your mind."

Agnes tried to calm down and focus, but her body was trembling with fear. But when Finias pulled her close and held her, her breathing slowed, and she could finally think clearly. She opened her mind to her daughters and saw each one, sound asleep safely in their beds.

She looked up at Finias. "But how?" she asked.

"Anyone who knows you knows that you would do anything to keep your daughters safe," he said. "What better way to get you to leave the safely of the property than to make you think one of them was in trouble."

She closed her eyes in self-recrimination. "And I nearly fell for it," she said, shaking her head. "How stupid…"

Finias put his hand under her chin and lifted her face up. "Agnes, look at me," he asked.

She opened her eyes, but they were filled with regret. "I'm so sorry…"

"You have nothing to be sorry about," he said. "You were defending your children. We've all been on edge, worrying about something happening. You just reacted as a momma wolf." He paused after he said those words. "Where's Fuzzy?"

"Fuzzy?" Agnes exclaimed. "I didn't even realize… He would have never…"

She turned and ran back towards the house, and Finias ran alongside her. They dashed up the stairs, through the front door and to Agnes' bedroom where Fuzzy lay, motionless on the bed.

"Oh, no," Agnes exclaimed. "Not Fuzzy!"

She ran to her wolf and felt for a pulse, then she looked up at Finias. "There's a pulse," she said, her eyes filled with tears. "But it's so weak."

"I'll get help!" Finias promised.

Chapter Forty

Rowan, Henry, and Seamus surrounded Fuzzy and slowly worked their way through his internal systems, trying to discover what had happened to him. Fuzzy whimpered softly and tried to lick Rowan's hand. Rowan placed her head against the wolf's head and breathed softly, pushing out calming thoughts to the distressed dog. Fuzzy sighed softly and relaxed. Then Rowan continued her part of the examination.

"There's something in his stomach," Rowan said "It looks like raw beef. Did he get any raw beef today?"

Agnes, tears in her eyes, shook her head, then spoke. "No," she said, taking a deep breath to try and calm her voice. "No, he just had his usual kibble."

"So, the beef may be the culprit," Rowan replied. "Hazel and Cat, can you come over here and help me?"

They both hurried to her sister's side. "Okay, this is going to sound weird," she said. "But Cat, I need you to connect Hazel to my thoughts. Then Hazel, when you see

281

what I'm seeing, I need you to take the meat out of Fuzzy stomach and put it…"

She paused and looked at her mother. Agnes ran over to her dresser, picked up a colorful ceramic dish that held various knickknacks, dumped the items onto the top of her dresser, and ran back with the dish. "Here," she said. "You can put it in here."

Rowan nodded. "And put it in there," she finished.

Hazel nodded. "Okay, I'm ready," she said, closing her eyes and waiting for Cat to make the connection.

Cat stood between her sisters and put a hand on each one's shoulder, then she closed her eyes and focused on becoming a conduit for their thoughts. Hazel had been focusing on keeping her thoughts clear when suddenly she could see vital organs all around her. "This is so cool," she said. "It's like one of those National Geographic specials. So, what am I seeing?"

"I'm taking you down past Fuzzy's heart and lungs to his stomach," Rowan said. "We'll pass through the stomach wall, and you'll see a disgusting conglomeration of partially digested food. The chunks of meat are what I really want."

Hazel nodded. "Could the poison have leached out of the meat?" she asked.

Rowan sighed. "Yes. Yes, it could have," she agreed. "Some of it has already entered his blood stream and caused this reaction."

"I'm going to take all the stuff out of the stomach, okay?" Hazel asked.

"Good idea," Rowan said.

Hazel concentrated on the contents of the stomach and then envisioned the ceramic dish. She waved her arm, and she could see the Fuzzy stomach was now empty. And the smell spreading throughout the room told her that the dish was now full.

She coughed a few times, then tried to concentrate again. "Do you need anything else?" she asked, hoping her sensitive pregnant stomach wouldn't react to the smell.

"No, I'm good," she said. "Thank you."

Cat lifted her hand from their shoulders, and the sisters opened their eyes. "I'll take the dish over to the lab and see if I can determine what the poison was," Rowan said.

"Send back some milk thistle," Seamus requested. "It looks like his liver has been affected by the poison."

Rowan nodded. "Hazel, why don't you come with me?" she suggested. "Then, you can send back the milk thistle immediately."

"I'll go too," Joseph said. "Just in case someone is still out there looking for trouble."

They hurried to the Still Room. Rowan unlocked the door and let them inside. She hurried across the lab to the apothecary and took a small bottle off one of the shelves. "Here," she said, giving it to Hazel. "Send this back to Seamus."

Before Rowan was able to hand it to Hazel, the bottle was gone. She smiled at her sister. "That was fast," she said.

Hazel shrugged. "It's Fuzzy," she said. "We have to save him."

Rowan took the dish over to the lab and put it down on a stainless-steel table. "This is going to take me a little while," she said. "If you need to go back…"

Hazel shook her head. "No, I'm okay," she said. "And I'm not going to leave you alone."

Joseph slowly scanned the building. "I can't see how anyone could be hiding inside," he said.

Rowan shook her head. "After Buck broke in," she said. "Henry and I worked on some pretty powerful spells to protect the area, as well as reinforcing the doors and windows with iron."

Joseph nodded in appreciation. "Nice job," he said. "So, would you mind if I walked around outside to see if I can find any evidence?"

"Go," Hazel said. "We're good."

285

"I'll only be a call away," he said, studying her eyes to make sure she wasn't feeling nervous about being left alone.

"I know," she said, meeting his gaze squarely. "We'll be fine."

Chapter Forty-one

Joseph jogged past the house and to the property line where Finias had found Agnes. He carefully inspected the area, walking slowly up the tree line and shining his flashlight several feet in both directions. He stopped when he arrived at the road and had found no evidence.

He turned back and took a deep breath, then he closed his eyes and concentrated on the wolf that dwelt inside of him. Soon, his breathing became labored, and his body began to change. The bones of his face began to elongate, his shoulders swelled in size, and hair began to cover his body. In a few moments, he lifted his head and howled at the night sky. Then, using his keen sense of smell and night vision, he slowly went back along the path he'd just traveled.

A few yards into his inspection, his nose caught the scent of raw meat. He followed the scent and found a crumpled piece of butcher's paper underneath an old pine tree. He looked closer and noticed white powder on the edges of the paper. The edges, he assumed, that Fuzzy hadn't licked clean.

Arsenic, he decided.

He carefully picked up the paper and folded it, so the powder was trapped inside, then he turned to go back to the Still Room with the evidence when another scent caught his attention.

He stopped and turned back, slowly advancing on the scent. He stared into the woods, studying each tree and bush with cautious vigilance. He growled, deep in his throat, as he got closer to the scent.

He stepped over the boundary and walked just on the other side of the tree line to an old oak. The scent was strongest here. He looked at the base of the tree and could see footprints embedded in the soft soil. He smelled the tree trunk and could smell the oil from the human's hand. Then he saw the coil of rope. He bent to study it and, as he moved, kicked a knife that had been hidden in the grass below the tree. Using the folded paper, he picked up the knife and then scooped the rope over his arm.

He slowly stood and scanned further out, growling menacingly. He could still pick up the scent of the intruder in the wind, and he longed to chase him down. But he knew that it was more important to get the paper to Rowan. So, he turned and ran back to the Still Room.

He pushed the Still Room door open and charged inside.

Hazel spun towards the door; her arms immediately locked into a defensive stance. Then she saw Joseph and relaxed. Rowan looked up at the same time and immediately gasped in surprise, then she exhaled loudly. "Sorry, Joseph," she breathed. "I'm just not used to you appearing as a Wulffolk."

Joseph began to change back into his human form. "Sorry," he said to both women, his voice still a low growl. "I was in such a hurry, I forgot who I was."

"It's okay," Hazel replied. "Fast is good in this circumstance. What did you find?"

He came over and placed the paper on her table. "I found this out in the woods, just on the other side of the property line," he said. "It smelled of raw meat, but I think the powder I found on it might be of more interest."

Rowan opened the paper and examined the powder. "Arsenic?" she guessed.

"That's what I thought, too," he said. "So, at least we know what he used."

"We'll need to cleanse his blood and organs," Rowan said, getting up from the desk and hurrying toward the door. "Thank you, Joseph, you may have just saved Fuzzy's life."

They all hurried out of the building and ran back to the house. "It's arsenic," Rowan called, rushing through the great room towards her mother's bedroom. "He was poisoned with arsenic."

Hazel stopped in the great room and turned to Joseph, stepping over to him and linking her arms around his neck. "Thank you," she said, her voice a little shaky. "Thank you for finding it."

He leaned forward and kissed her tenderly. "Well, you know, Fuzzy and I are part of the same pack," he said. "We have to look out for each other."

She smiled up at him. "I love you," she said.

He kissed her again. "I love you too."

Chapter Forty-two

Wanda finished packing her second suitcase early the next morning. She looked around her bedroom, making sure she took everything she was going to need. Everything she wanted in case she never came back to Whitewater. On top of her dresser was a framed photograph of her mother. She walked across the room and picked it up, studying her mother's face and noting the similarities between them. But also, for the first time, seeing the sadness in her mother's eyes.

Her mother's death had been another reason she'd grown up hating the Willoughbys. Her father had always told her that it was their fault that she had died. He told her that he'd pleaded with them to help her, but they refused. Said that she hadn't been part of their coven, so she was out of luck.

For the first time in her life, she questioned her father's words. She had never known any of the Willoughbys to refuse help to someone in need. Even though they were sworn enemies, she had secretly admired their empathy and compassion. Could her father have lied to her?

She turned the frame over. The cardboard on the back was brittle and discolored. Carefully, she twisted the small nails, so they released the backing, and she carefully lifted the cardboard out of the frame to get to the photo. The cellophane tape holding the photo to the matting was yellowed and crumbling. Wanda loosened it with her fingernail and was able to pull the photo free.

A date was written that was only a few months before her mother's death, and it was the only thing she had left of her mother. Her father had gotten rid of everything else soon after her mother had passed way. He said he didn't want to be reminded of her, it hurt him too much.

"That's fine for him," she murmured, walking back to her bed and sitting down with the photo in her hands. "But he left me without anything to hold onto. He only worried about his grief, not mine."

293

She placed one hand on the front of the photo and one hand on the back, then she closed her eyes and let her mind empty.

She could see the living room in the old house they lived in when she was young. The house that smelled like flowers and homemade cookies. She felt a wave of peace fall over her, she was home. The last real home she remembered.

Looking around she saw her mother, lying on the couch, with a blanket over her. She remembered her mother doing that for months before she passed away.

"Please, Wade," her mother was saying to her father. "Please, just let her come. She said she could help me."

"We don't need no Willoughbys helping us," Wade stated, folding his arms over his chest. "You're gonna be just fine. You just need to rest."

"I need more than rest, Wade," she pleaded. "And Agnes said that she would be happy to help. It wouldn't cost..."

"You think I want their charity?" Wade yelled.
"You think I want to be in debt to those holier-than-thou
Willoughbys?"

"Wade, I need their help," she continued. "I don't
want to die."

He turned on her, his face red with anger. "You
ain't gonna die," he shouted. "You hear that! You just get
that idea out of your head. You ain't gonna die. And we
ain't gonna call any Willoughbys over to pretend to help.
This discussion is over!"

He stormed out of the house, slamming the door
so hard, the flower vases rattled inside the house.

Wanda opened her eyes and brushed away the
tears. Another lie. All this hate she'd had for the
Willoughbys had been based on another lie. Her father had
killed her mother, his stupid pride had killed her mother.

She stood up and put the photo back in the frame,
placed the cardboard on top of it, and readjusted the nails,
so they held everything in place. Then she put the frame
in her suitcase, protected by several layers of clothing.

She closed the lid and snapped the lock shut. "Good-bye, Daddy," she said angrily. "Have a good life."

Pulling the suitcase off the bed, she paused when her phone vibrated, announcing a text message. She dropped the suitcase on the floor and reached across the bed for her purse that held her phone. She pulled it out of the outside pocket and looked at the message.

"I need my medicine. I got some at the old place. Bring them to the cabin. Dad."

"You can go to hell," she said to the phone and stuffed it back into her purse. She pulled both suitcases out of the bedroom and to the front door, turning off all the lights in the apartment as she went through. She picked up the mail that was lying on the floor in front of the door and shrugged. "I guess the good thing about running away is that I won't be getting any more junk mail," she said, flipping through the catalogs and letters in her hand. She tossed the entire pile into a wastebasket near the front door and shrugged. She wasn't going to leave a forwarding address because she didn't really know where she was going, and she didn't want anyone to find out where she'd gone.

She opened her door, pulled the suitcases out behind her, tucking them behind the porch railing so they wouldn't be seen, and then locked the door. Glancing up and down the street, she waited while a car drove past her house and turned at the next corner before pulling the suitcases down the steps to her car. Knowing that most of her neighbors worked during the day, she felt the only threat of being discovered was from someone driving down her street.

And she wanted to be sure no one saw her leave with suitcases.

She quickly stashed her luggage into her trunk, threw her purse onto the passenger seat of the car, and climbed into the drivers' seat. As she put the key into the ignition, her phone chimed again, alerting her of another message. She paused, her hands on ten and two, and stared out her windshield to the building in front of her.

"I don't need to look," she said aloud. "I'm leaving. I don't care who's messaging me."

She put her hand back on the key, and the phone chimed again.

"Dammit," she muttered, leaning over and pulling her phone from the pocket of her purse.

"I'm not feeling too well, but Ben's making us go out again. If you could just leave my meds on the kitchen counter, that would be great. Dad."

"No," she yelled at the phone. "No, I am not getting your pills."

An image of her father clutching his heart and falling to the floor of the cabin flashed through her mind. She didn't hate him. Try as she might, she couldn't hate him. She just didn't like him very much.

"But I don't want it to be my fault that he dies," she said with a sigh. "Fine. I'll get the damn pills."

Chapter Forty-three

Even though she had made her body invisible, Wanda still hurried out of her father's house, down the alley, and slipped into her car, sliding the paper sack of pill bottles underneath her purse before she reversed the spell and was visible again. She'd parked a half-block away from the house and used a parking lot belonging to an apartment building, so her car wouldn't be detected if they were monitoring his home. Once inside the house, it had been easy to find the old containers of pills on his nightstand next to his bed. Now, all she wanted to do was to drop off the medicine and get on the road.

She glanced around, making sure there was no one in the vicinity, and then pulled out of the parking lot. Taking a deep breath and exhaling slowly, she tried to relax. But she knew the police would come around soon, questioning her about the escape. It wasn't if they were going to come after her, but when.

She pushed the button on her car radio for the local news channel, just to see if there were any updates on the escape.

The family of a Chicago couple camping in the Kettle Moraine area have asked local residents to help them locate the missing couple. Emma and Hugh O'Keefe had told their families they would be returning to Chicago last night, but no one has been able to contact them, and local rangers found their campsite empty. Emma is about five foot, four inches tall with light, brown hair. Hugh is five foot, eight inches tall with dark brown hair. The couple, who are in their twenties, were driving a light blue Subaru Forester with an Illinois license plate. If you see anyone matching their description, please call the Whitewater Police Department.

Wanda shrugged. They probably just decided to extend their stay and discovered there was no cell service, she thought. It happened all the time.

She listened to the rest of the news and discovered there were no updates on the escaped prisoners. From the news report, they were still searching for them up in the Upper Peninsula of Michigan. She breathed another sigh of relief. "Good," she whispered.

She finally came to the road that ran in front of the cabin. She paused at the intersection, looking all ways to make sure no one was following her, then she proceeded forward. She drove past the cabin and pulled to the side of the road that was almost completely hidden by brush.

Picking up the bag, she exited the car and walked through the woods to the back of the cabin. She retrieved the key from underneath the planter and then jogged to the garage door. After opening the door, she stepped inside the garage and closed the door before reaching over and turning on the light. She was a little surprised to see a car parked in the garage.

"If you've got a car, why the hell couldn't you get your own damn pills?" she muttered.

She walked around the car and headed to the door that led to the kitchen. She reached for the doorknob, but when she heard loud voices coming from inside, she stopped.

"The Master is well pleased with our offering," she could hear Ben say. "The innocent blood spilled yesterday gave him much needed strength."

Blood? she questioned. *What did they kill?*

"We ain't gonna have to do that again, are we?" her father asked.

"We will do whatever the Master needs us to do," Ben yelled. "Do you have a problem with that?"

"No!" Wade stammered. "You know, it's just that we don't have a whole lot of places to hide their cars. That garage can't fit more than just one car at a time."

Wanda slowly turned and looked at the car behind her. It was a light blue Subaru Forester, like the one described on the news. She glanced around the room and saw a few towels that hadn't been there before. She put the bag of pills on the counter next to the door and quietly walked over to the towels and picked one up.

The large colorful beach towel had splotches of rust-colored stains all over it. She fisted the towel in her hand and closed her eyes. A moment later, her eyes wide with horror, she dropped the towel, holding her hand over her mouth to hold in the scream that wanted so desperately to escape. She took a deep, shuddering breath and forced herself to calm down. She needed to leave, quietly, because she had no doubt in her mind that if Ben could read her thoughts, she would be the next one to be murdered for the Master.

She moved quietly, but as quickly as she could to the door. Only then did she remember the pills. If she left them there, they would know she'd seen the car. She reached out her hand, and the bag levitated and made its way across the garage to her. She grabbed it, turned off the light, and stepped out of the garage.

Leaning against the garage wall, she took another deep breath as she tried to decide what to do. At this point, if she didn't deliver the pills, they would be suspicious. But there was no way she could enter that cabin and not

303

have her face give away her complete fear and disgust at what they'd done. For a moment, she was frozen with fear, her heart pounding in her chest and breath coming out in quiet gasps.

Finally, she gave herself a mental shake, any one of them could leave the cabin at any time and catch her while she tried to make up her mind about what to do.

"My car," she whispered. "I need to get back to my car."

She quietly jogged back to the woods and made her way back to the road through the forest. The garage blocked any view from the cabin on that side of the house. When she got parallel to the front of the cabin, she levitated the bag of pills across the front yard and set them behind a ceramic flowerpot near the front door. Then she turned herself invisible as she traversed the final yards back to the road and her car.

She got into her car, pulled out her phone, and texted her father.

"Your pills are in a bag near the front door. I thought someone might be following me, so I didn't want to risk getting too close to the cabin. When I pulled out, they were nowhere to be seen, so I was probably just being over cautious."

A moment later, she received a text back.

"Ben said you were smart for not stopping."

"Yeah, well, I'm thrilled to hear what Ben thinks," she muttered, turning on her car and driving away from the cabin. "But I don't think Ben is going to like what I'm going to do next."

She waited until she was several miles away from the cabin, and then she said, "Siri, call Donovan Farrington."

Her phone responded. "Calling Donovan Farrington."

Chapter Forty-four

Donovan hung up his phone and looked around the yard where the rest of their group was playing fetch with Fuzzy. The huge wolf was happily running from one person to the next, but he was a little slower than usual.

"I know how you're feeling," Donovan muttered, still recovering from the infection the demon had given him the day before.

He strolled toward the group and stopped alongside Cat, placing his arm around her shoulders. She smiled up at him, her heart in her eyes. "Hi," she said. "How are you feeling?"

"Much better than yesterday," he said. "But still a little slower than usual. How's Fuzzy doing?"

"Great," she said with a wide smile. "He's so much better. I was so worried…"

She paused and took a deep breath, then shook her head. "But, he's good," she added. "He's great."

Donovan looked over to where Fuzzy and Joseph were now wrestling in the grass, over who got the ball. "I think Fuzzy's got this," he laughed.

"Unless Joseph goes full Wulffolk on us," Cat agreed.

Donovan turned to her. "I need to talk to you about a phone call I just got," he said.

"Sure," she replied, turning and letting him guide her away from the family. "What's up?"

"Wanda just called me," he said. "She sounded really upset. I've never heard her sound this way."

"What happened to her?" Cat asked.

He shrugged. "She didn't want to say over the phone," he replied. "She wanted to meet with me, so I told her to come here."

Cat nodded slowly, digesting the information for a long moment. "You know we think it was Ben who not only tried to kidnap Mom last night, but he also poisoned Fuzzy," she said. "How do we know this isn't a trick?"

"We don't," he said. "And you're exactly right. Wanda has never been on our side. But, the tone of her voice…she was scared. No, terrified."

"When is she coming?" Cat asked.

Donovan winced slightly. "She's on her way now," he said.

"And what if I had said no, she can't come?" she asked.

"I would have called her back and told her that I would meet her someone where else," he replied immediately. "This isn't a game, Cat. I really do think she's in trouble."

Cat nodded. "Okay, well, then we should tell the rest of the family, so they can be prepared too."

They walked back over to the group, and Donovan called out, "Hey, could we all just gather together for a moment. I have something I need to tell you."

Henry ran over to Rowan, put his arm around her shoulders, and together, they walked toward Donovan and

Cat. Hazel walked over to Joseph, who was still on the ground and helped him up, then they, along with Fuzzy joined the group. Dustin and Seamus jogged over from the opposite side of the yard. But Finias and Agnes took their time.

"You seem worried," Finias said softly to Agnes.

She looked up to the sky and then nodded. "I feel like there's a shadow over us," she replied. "Like the other shoe is about to drop. Does that make sense?"

He nodded. "Perfect sense," he replied. "Did you dream last night?"

She closed her eyes and sighed, then turned to him. "Yes, I did," she said. "And once again, I was walking in a cemetery."

"Well, it could have been…" he began.

"Don't tell me that it could have been my reaction from what happened last night," she interrupted quietly. "I've had the same dream for weeks now."

He sighed. "So have I," he confessed. "And, you might as well know, Seamus and Dustin have had similar dreams."

Stopping just a few yards away from her gathering family, Agnes watched her daughters interact with the men they loved. She took a deep breath. "I would willingly die for them to have peace," she said softly.

"But wouldn't it be better if we could all live?" Finias replied softly.

Chapter Forty-five

Wanda pulled her car into the driveway of the Willoughby Farm and looked at the faces of all of those waiting to greet her. She nearly put the car in reverse and sped away.

"But where would I go?" she asked herself.

She slowed the car and pulled up next to the back porch, turned off the car and stepped out.

Agnes came down the steps with a smile on her face. "Wanda, welcome," she said, tucking her arm through Wanda's arm. "It's been such a long time since you were here. I'm so glad you could come."

"I was here?" Wanda asked, confused.

"Well, you were pretty small," Agnes admitted. "Your mother used to bring you here. You loved playing with Fuzzy."

"Fuzzy?" she asked.

Suddenly, the giant wolf bounded down the stairs towards them. Wanda froze, panic rising in her throat, as

311

Fuzzy loped closer. She expected the animal to attack or, at the very least, to growl at her. But instead, the wolf dropped to its haunches in front of her and smiled, its tongue lolling out of the side of his mouth, and its tail frantically whipping back and forth on the ground.

"It looks like Fuzzy remembers you," Agnes said with a smile.

Wanda slipped her arm from within Agnes' arm and squatted down in front of the large canine. "I do remember," she whispered softly, tentatively reaching out to touch Fuzzy's soft muzzle. "I remember playing with him in the lavender fields."

Agnes chuckled. "That's right," she said. "You girls would play hide and seek in the fields with Fuzzy. But your giggles would always give you away."

Wanda looked up and met Hazel's eyes. "You were right," she said. "We were friends."

Hazel nodded and smiled. "I forgive you for not coming to my birthday party," she teased. "Do you want to come in?"

Wanda stood up and nodded. "I would like that," she said. "I'd like that very much."

They entered the house, and Agnes led her to the dining room table. "This is where we have most of our family counsels," she said. "Please have a seat. Would you like something? Water? Tea?"

"Water would be nice," Wanda replied, sitting at the table and folding her hands in front of her. "Although, after you hear what I'm going to say, you probably won't want me hanging around."

Agnes brought a glass of water over and set it in front of Wanda. "Why don't you tell us, and let us decide," she suggested, slipping into the adjacent chair.

"First, I don't know if Donovan told you or not, but I helped my father and the rest of them escape from prison," she said, then she glanced over at Joseph. "I guess this is on the record now."

He shook his head. "Let's say this is part of a family meeting for now," he suggested. "We can talk about it on the record later."

313

She nodded. "So, Ben gave me specific directions about what he wanted and how I should bring it to them in prison," she explained. "I brought plastic explosives that could destroy the locks on the cells, so they could escape. Then I waited outside one of the doors. Ben and the rest made themselves invisible and got into my car while I spoke with one of the guards who was off-duty and was on his way home." She paused and took a deep shuddering breath. "Then Ben killed him. Choked him. For no reason. He couldn't see Ben or anyone. He wasn't even on duty."

"What did you do?" Agnes said.

"I got into the car and drove," Wanda said. "I guess I was scared, because if Ben would do this to someone who posed no threat, what would he do to me?"

"That makes sense," Hazel said. "I think I would have been frightened too."

Wanda sent Hazel a smile of gratitude. "Thanks," she said. "Then I dropped them off at a cabin near Kettle Moraine. I'd stopped on the way at a gas station and got some things for them for overnight. But my dad had given me a list of other things they wanted the next day."

Hazel nodded. "That's when I saw you at the store, right?"

"Right," she replied. "I brought the groceries, but no one was there. Then I found a note from my dad telling me that I didn't need to stay. I held on to the note, so I could get an impression of what was going on in the room when it was written."

"You can do that?" Cat asked. "Pick up impressions from inanimate objects?"

"Yes," Wanda replied slowly. "Can't everyone?"

Cat shook her head. "No, that's a unique gift," she said. "But, sorry for interrupting, go on."

"I could tell that Ben was angry and that he didn't trust me. He thought that I was soft because I had objected to the murder of the guard," she explained. "I felt like I was expendable, and it scared me, so I got out of there. I saw Donovan after that, and he could tell that I was upset.

315

I gave him the information about the cabin, and he suggested that I leave town."

"Why didn't you?" Joseph asked.

"I planned to," she replied. "I called a friend who lived out of town, and I was going to stay with her until I could figure out what to do next. I packed my stuff and I was heading out when I got a text from my dad." She looked around the table at all of the people sitting there. "I would have ignored it, but he needed his medications and I didn't want his death on my hands."

"That makes sense," Joseph said.

"So, I went to his house, got the medications," she said, then she turned to Joseph. "Oh, if you had someone watching his house, I made myself invisible, so they wouldn't have seen me."

"Another great talent," Cat added.

"So, I went back to the cabin and let myself in through the garage door," Wanda said. "The first thing I noticed was that they had a car in the garage. Then I overheard them inside the cabin arguing, so I didn't want to go in and get caught up in that. Then I noticed some towels on the garage floor that hadn't been there before. They had a rust-colored stain on them."

"Blood," Joseph said.

Wanda nodded slowly. "Yes," she said, her voice shaking. "It was the missing campers, from Chicago. They killed them."

Chapter Forty-six

"The missing couple from Chicago?" Joseph asked.

Wanda nodded. "I had the radio on when I was driving to the cabin," she said. "And I heard the announcement. I blew it off because there are always bulletins like that. But the car matched the description of their car and the towels…"

She took a deep breath and tried to continue, but words just wouldn't form. Her breath came out as gasps, and she felt her chest constricting as the horror of what she'd seen overwhelmed her. Agnes put her arms around her and held her for a few moments. "That's okay," she whispered calmly. "You just take your time."

It had been a long time since anyone had offered her that kind of motherly comfort, so Wanda allowed herself to absorb the kindness and sympathy offered for a few moments. Then she sat up and wiped the tears from her cheeks. "Thank you," she said to Agnes.

Then she turned to Joseph. "When I held the towels, I was able to see what they did to them," she said. "They took them from their campsite and waited until late in the evening. Then they brought them to the large black rock above the lake."

"We know the place," Hazel said.

"They waited until midnight, they laid them on the rock and killed them," she said. She shook her head. "No, they sacrificed them. Ben kept saying that it's what the demon needed to become stronger." She shuddered and took another deep breath. "They waited until all of their blood drained down through a crevice in the rock. The crevice glowed red for a few moments, then everything was quiet."

"Well, that explains the increase of the demon's power," Donovan said. "And you were right about Ben being dangerous."

"Wanda, this talent you have, being able to get impressions," Joseph said, standing up and walking across the room to a box. "Can I give you something I found and see if you can get an impression from it?"

She nodded. "Sure, I can try."

Joseph picked up the length of rope he'd found under the tree the night before and brought it over to her. "What do you get from this?" he asked.

She held the rope in her hand and closed her eyes. Her hand shook at the image of Ben immediately appeared. "It belongs to Ben," she said, still concentrating on the impressions. "He's hiding in the woods, waiting for someone. He has a knife, too." She took a deep breath. "He's waiting for her with a mixture of desire and hate. He wants to rape her, but he also wants to kill her, slowly and painfully."

Agnes gasped softly and leaned back in her chair, her face pale. Wanda opened her eyes and turned to Agnes. "You," she breathed, her eyes wide with understanding. "He was trying to kill you."

Agnes nodded slowly. "Yes," she said, her voice shaking. "But he wasn't able to do it. And now, thanks to you, we know what he was up to."

"And since he was hunting for you last night," Joseph said. "They probably weren't hunting anyone else."

"But does that mean they'll be hunting someone today?" Hazel asked. "There's only one more night until Samhain. Wouldn't the demon want even more power?"

"I need to find out," Joseph said.

"I'll go with you," Donovan offered.

Joseph turned to Donovan and shook his head. "Not that I wouldn't want you on my side," he said. "But, you're too big a blip on the demon's radar right now."

"But they could be anywhere," Wanda said. "If they're hunting, they're not going to be at the cabin. And, if they're at the cabin, they are going to be prepared for you."

"Ben's probably stronger, too," Agnes added. "What he did last night, that took some power that Ben

321

didn't have. We need to be sure that we're coming from a position of power."

"We need to go to the rock," Hazel said. "And we need to be waiting for them tonight."

"Hazel's right," Finias agreed. "And we all need to be there. We need to fight together."

Chapter Forty-seven

"I need innocent blood," Ben snarled quietly at Wade as they watched the six-year-old twin girls throw pebbles into the river. They had blonde hair, pulled into pigtails, and were wearing pink sweatshirts and blue jeans.

They looked just like Wanda did when she was their age, Wade thought. It made him feel sick to his stomach to even think about taking them. "But Ben, they're just kids," Wade argued. "They ain't done nothing to no one."

"You don't understand," Ben whispered angrily. "It's a privilege, an honor to be sacrificed for a cause like this. The Master, once he defeats the Willoughbys, will rise up, a benevolent deity who will rule us all."

"But, Ben, couldn't we just find someone else?" Wade pleaded. "Like, you know, some lambs. Lambs make good sacrifices. It's, you know, symbolic and everything."

"Those two crossing our path means they were meant to be our final sacrifice for the Master," Ben said. He turned and glared at Wade, his eyes suddenly glowing red. "Do you understand?"

Wade swallowed audibly and nodded. "Yeah, I guess," he said. "But…"

"Do you want to die along with them?" Ben asked.

Wade shook his head. "No. No, of course not," he said.

"Then, use your magic and help me capture them."

With a sad sigh, Wade turned and concentrated on a spot a little further up the river from where the girls were playing. Suddenly, a puppy appeared at the edge of the river, splashing in the water and barking in delight.

"Look!" one of the girls exclaimed. "A puppy!"

The other looked around the area. "I don't see its owner," she said. "Maybe it's lost."

"And coyotes could eat it if we don't help it," the first one theorized.

"Should we tell Dad?" the second one asked.

The first one shook her head. "No, let's make it a surprise," she said with a wide smile.

"Puppy!" they called. "Puppy! Puppy!"

The puppy barked at them, wagged his tail, and ran further up the river. The girls followed it, staying on the sandy bank as they traveled. "Puppy!! Come back here," the first one called. She turned to her sister. "Do you have any treats?"

Her sister shook her head. "No, we ate all the cookies before we got to the river," she replied. Then she looked ahead. "I can't see the puppy anymore. We should run."

The girls ran further down the river, away from the campground, and into the woods. "Puppy! Puppy!!" they called as they ducked beneath long-hanging tree branches and climbed over large logs.

The puppy barked once again, further away, and the girls continued their search. Finally, when they were more than a mile away from the campground, they stopped. Tired and disappointed, they sat on a large log near the riverbank.

"I guess we should go back now," the first one said. "Maybe Daddy could get the car and drive us around to find the puppy."

Her sister nodded. "That's a good idea," she said. "I'm tired and hungry."

Just then, Ben stepped out of the forest and onto the riverbank. "Hello girls," he said.

The girls jumped up and backed away from him.

"I'm sorry," he said, pasting on a phony smile. "I've been looking for my puppy, and I can't find him anywhere. You didn't happen to see him, did you?"

Still fearful, but concerned about the puppy, the girls nodded.

"We saw him," the first one said. "He went down the river."

326

Ben pointed in the direction they'd come from. "That way?" he asked.

The girls shook their heads. "No," the second one said, pointing past Ben. "He went that way."

"Thank you," he replied, nodding, then he turned and called in the direction. "Wade! Puppy! Herc boy!"

The puppy appeared a few yards ahead, barking and splashing in the water. Ben smiled at the girls. "You saved my puppy," he said. "I was really worried about him."

The first girl shrugged her shoulders. "We didn't do anything," she said. "He just came when you called."

"Yeah," her sister agreed. "He wouldn't even come to us."

"Would you like to pet him?" Ben asked.

The sisters looked at each other and, with that silent language that only twins understand, decided immediately that they didn't want to stay any longer.

"No, thank you," the first sister said. "We need to get back to our campsite."

327

"Thanks anyway," the second one added.

They turned around and froze when they saw Buck and Nelson behind them.

"I'm sorry," Ben whispered in their ears. "I'm afraid I'm going to have to insist."

Chapter Forty-eight

A fire crackled in the stone fireplace, soft music played in the background, and Agnes sat with her daughters and Wanda, sipping mugs of fragrant tea in the living room. The sun was starting to lower in the sky, and a chill was in the air.

"So, did you find your wedding dress?" Cat asked her mother. "Tomorrow is Samhain."

Agnes nodded. "Actually, I did find it," she said. "And it still fits."

"Go, Mom," Hazel said with a smile. "Although I didn't doubt it for a minute."

Wanda put her tea mug on the end table next to her. "I can't believe you're getting married in the midst of all of this," Wanda said as she sat with the sisters in the great room.

"We need to find joy in the moment," Cat said. "And there's no more powerful force on earth than love."

"But what about your reception?" Wanda asked. "What about guests? What about a photographer?"

Rowan laughed. "I think we'll be a little busy right after the handfasting to worry too much about those things," she said. "The idea is to be sure we are bound together with the people we love. Everything else is not important."

"But, you know, we'll have food," Hazel said. "Afterwards. I have it all planned out."

"Afterwards?" Wanda exclaimed.

Hazel nodded. "Oh, yeah, I totally plan on kicking demon butt and then coming home and feasting," she replied. "You're invited."

"Okay, I'll be there," Wanda promised. "After we kick demon butt."

Surprised, Rowan looked over at Wanda. "I have to admit that I'm a little surprised by that," she said. "Why do you want to help us fight the demon? I mean, I get that you want to stop Ben and the rest, but this demon thing is our fight."

Wanda shook her head. "No, it's my fight, too," she said. "It was my ancestor who messed things up. My ancestor who gave the demon more strength to fight. And, besides, my mom's side of the family was part of your coven. She was a cousin way back, so I guess this is my fight too."

"We're glad to have you, cousin," Hazel teased, then her smile disappeared. "I'm really sorry that we didn't do this sooner."

"Yeah, me too," Wanda agreed sadly. "I always thought you guys were the enemy. I had no idea until this morning that you were actually my friends."

"This morning?" Agnes asked. "What happened this morning?"

"I took my mom's photo out of the frame that it's been in for years," Wanda explained. "I held it to get an impression and discovered that my mom wanted to come and see you when she was sick, but my dad wouldn't let her."

Agnes sighed. "I always wondered why she didn't come," she said. "I actually went to her, but your father wouldn't let me in."

Wanda closed her eyes, trying to fight the rage inside of her. "I hate him," she said softly.

Agnes leaned towards her and placed her hand on Wanda's arm. "No, don't hate him," she said. "I'm sure that he was being pressured, and he probably thought he was protecting both of you."

"Who would have pressured him?" Wanda asked, confused.

"Ben was the head of the coven," Agnes said. "And Ben has never had any use for the Willoughbys. He probably threatened your father."

"He should have been stronger," Wanda said.

Agnes shrugged and nodded. "I agree, but some people just don't have that kind of courage in them," she said. "They would rather go with the flow than stand up and fight."

"I'm his daughter," Wanda argued. "And I would have fought."

Agnes smiled at her. "You are like your mother," she said. "And she would have fought too. But she was too tired to keep fighting."

"I just wish…" Wanda began but stopped when Joseph rushed into the room.

"We need to get ready," he said urgently.

Hazel sat up, putting her mug on the coffee table. "What's wrong? What happened?"

"Two little girls, six-year-old twins, are missing from one of the campgrounds," he said, his face grave.

"Ben," Wanda said.

Joseph nodded. "Yeah, that's what I think, too," he said.

"Well, let's go get them now," Hazel said, standing up. "We don't have to wait until tonight. We know where they are."

"And he will kill them if he thinks he's compromised," Wanda said. "Or, he'll move them somewhere else."

Cat nodded. "The stone is probably the most powerful place for a sacrifice," she said, "as far as the demon is concerned, but there are probably other places they could perform it."

"I could flash in, grab them, and flash out," Hazel said.

"No!" Joseph exclaimed. "Ben has become stronger, and we don't know what his powers are like. He might be able to catch you and we're not going to risk that."

Hazel opened her mouth to argue, but Wanda stopped her. "He's right," she said. "Ben is basically a conduit for the demon now. No one should face him alone. We need to present a united front."

Chapter Forty-nine

Agnes glanced over at the clock on her nightstand. It was nearly eight-thirty, and they were planning on leaving the house at nine. She pulled her black turtleneck over her head and tucked it into her black jeans, then she sat on the edge of her bed to pull on her black hiking boots. As she pulled on the first one, she heard a light tapping on her bedroom door.

"Yes?" she called.

"May I come in?" Finias asked.

"Yes, come in," she replied.

He opened the door and quickly closed it behind himself.

He took her breath away, she decided, looking at him dressed in all black, his sweatshirt stretched over his muscular chest and arms, and his dark jeans emphasizing the length and strength of his legs. He walked across the room and sat down next to her on the bed.

"Agnes, I don't want you to come tonight," he said evenly.

She was so caught up in her response to his appearance, that it took her a moment to register his words. "Excuse me?" she asked.

"I don't want you to come tonight," he said. "I want you to stay here, where it's safe."

"Safe," she repeated. "You want me to be safe?"

He sighed and nodded, misinterpreting her comment. "I knew you'd understand," he said.

She shook her head. "No, actually, I don't understand," she replied, shoving her other foot in her boot and lacing it angrily. "I have fought this fight all of my life. And you, who have been here for several weeks, have decided that I need to be safe?"

She finished tying her laces on the second boot and sat up, glaring at him. "This is my fight, Finias," she snapped. "My fight. My family. My daughters. I will not stay at home and be safe."

"But you don't understand," he replied, placing his hands on her shoulders. "Ben is obsessed with you. His animus for you exceeds all of the feelings he has for the rest of us. He will focus that hate on you."

She pulled away from him and bent down to lace the first boot. Trying to regain her composure before she said something that she'd regret later. *Finias is trying to be helpful*, she said to herself, *he is just being protective. He's being an ass!*

She sat up and faced him. "Do you want to know why Ben hates me?" she asked. "Do you want to know why his anger and frustration is focused on me?"

She stood up, faced Finias, and placed her hands on her hips. "From the moment I was in school, Ben Stoughton decided that he liked to use me as a verbal and sometimes physical punching bag. And I took it. An harm it none. He would rally other bullies around him, and they all thought that I was weak because I didn't fight back. Because in their world, fighting was the only way to show strength."

337

She took a deep breath and pushed her hair out of her face. "Finally, I had to fight," she continued. "Ben was in the process of raping a girl underneath the bleachers at a football game. I interceded and took him and Wade and Neal on. She got away, but then he grabbed me. He cast a spell that constricted my neck, so I was choking. And as he walked toward me, he told me about all the things he and his friends were going to do to me while I was unconscious. He made the mistake of using his hand to grope me, so the spell was broken."

Agnes was glad to see Finias' eyes widen, and anger stirring in their depths. "I had nearly blacked out," she said. "But that instant saved my life. I forgot about an harm it none. I wanted to kill him. I threw him against the bleachers. Then I threw Wade and Neal in the other direction. Then I picked Ben up and threw him against the bleachers again. I heard the crack of bone against metal. I saw his limp body fall to the ground. And I realized I had gone too far."

"What did you do?" Finias asked, his jaw tight with rage.

"I healed him," she replied. "I healed him, and then I warned him that if he ever did something like that to anyone else, I'd take his life back."

She stared at him for a long moment. Then she tossed her hair behind her shoulders. "Now, do you want to ask me again to stay home?" she asked.

He stood up and walked over to her, placing his hands on her shoulders once again. "No," he said simply. "All I ask is that you give me an opportunity to punish him too."

She exhaled slowly and then smiled. "This isn't about revenge, Finias," she reminded him.

He looked down at her, his eyes still filled with rage. "Now it is," he said simply. "Let's go."

Chapter Fifty

They drove slowly, following a park maintenance access road that was barely more than a dirt trail. Joseph led the caravan, more familiar with the area than the rest of the group. Finally, he pulled the car into a small clearing, and the rest of the cars followed.

"Where are we?" Hazel asked.

"The lake and the rock are about two miles away, down this path," Joseph said. "We can use the cover of the woods to make it down there without being seen."

Donovan walked to the edge of the tree line and looked down the ravine. "I can see the rock from here," he said, keeping his voice low. "There's no sign of activity yet."

Joseph nodded. "It's only nine-thirty. I figured we could get down there and still have plenty of time to hide before they arrived."

"Okay," Henry said. "Then let's get…"

"Wait," Donovan called. "I see a car light approaching the lake."

Joseph jogged over and stood by Donovan; his eyes morphed from human to canine, and he stared down at the approaching car. "It's them, dammit," he growled.

Hazel came up behind them. "Where did you want us to hide?" she asked.

He scanned the area and saw several huge boulders, not far from the granite rock face. "Over there, behind those boulders," he said. "But now…"

"Everyone bunch together." Hazel said. "We're going for a ride."

"Can you do this?" Joseph asked as they moved together in a small clump.

She smiled at him. "Only one way to find out," she said. She closed her eyes and imagined the entire group behind the boulders Joseph had pointed out. She took a deep breath and waved her arms. When she opened them, they were all standing on the rough ground behind the boulders.

"How do you want this to go down?" Finias asked quietly.

"Hazel will grab the girls and bring them back here," Joseph replied. "At the moment, when they're confused, we come out pushing back with everything we've got. The purpose is to contain, not destroy." He looked slowly around the group. "Contain, not destroy."

Then he turned to Hazel. "Once you get the girls, get them back to the cars," he said. "In case something grows wrong, I don't want them available to the demon."

She nodded slowly. "But nothing's going to go wrong, right?" she whispered.

He sent her a half-smile. "Of course not," he replied. "I'm in charge."

"Wanda," Finias asked. "Can your father disappear too?"

She shook her head. "No, I got that from my mom," she explained. "My dad can create objects that look real but aren't."

"So, he could make a duplicate of one of us," Cat said.

Wanda nodded.

"Code word," Agnes said. "Daffodil."

"What?" Wanda asked.

"To prove it's really you," Agnes replied. "We'll ask for the code word. Daffodil."

"You couldn't have picked something more manly?" Seamus complained.

Agnes smiled. "They would have expected manly," she said.

Just then, they heard voices being carried on the night breeze, and they all were silent. Joseph slid alongside the boulder and watched them approach the rock face.

Wanda turned to Hazel. "Do you need to be able to see the girls in order to move them?" she whispered.

Hazel nodded.

"Duck behind me," Wanda whispered. "And I can get you a better view."

343

"How?" Hazel breathed.

"I don't disappear," she said. "I'm just camouflaged. So, if you're behind me, they can't see you either."

"Let's go," Hazel said.

Hazel moved behind Wanda and put her hands on Wanda's waist. Suddenly, she couldn't see Wanda any longer, but could still feel her beneath her hands.

"Ready?" Wanda asked.

"Yes," Hazel whispered. "Let's go."

They moved slowly to the side of the boulders, and Wanda stopped just alongside their hiding place. Hazel peered out through a small space between Wanda's arm and her waist. She shivered slightly when she looked at the black granite rock faced where she'd almost been killed only a few months earlier. "I can see it," Hazel breathed, her voice shaking.

"You okay?" Wanda whispered.

"Yeah, bad memories," Hazel said softly.

"I see them," Wanda whispered urgently. "It's

time."

Chapter Fifty-one

Wade looked down at the little girl in his arms, and his heart broke. Her eyes were wide with fear, her face tear-stained and the gag around her mouth seemed to be much too tight. "I'm sorry, sweetheart," he whispered.

She whimpered softly, and tears filled her eyes again. She struggled to free herself from his arms, but he tightened his hold and shook his head. "You can't get away," he said softly. "I'm so sorry. But you can't get away."

"What are you saying to her?" Ben growled.

Wade rolled his eyes and bit back his anger. "Nothing, okay?" he replied. "I'm just trying to calm her down a bit, so she's not scared."

Ben walked up next to Wade and looked down in the little girl's face and sneered. "She should be scared," he taunted. "I'm going to slit her neck from one side to the other."

The girl whimpered loudly, and tears poured down her cheeks.

"Why did you have to do that?" Wade seethed. "Why did you have to frighten her?"

Ben looked up at Wade, his eyes wild with madness, and smiled. "Because scaring them is half the fun," he replied.

Wade shook his head. "You've lost your soul, Ben," he said earnestly. "I'm afraid for you. You've lost all sense of what's good and right."

"I don't need a soul," Ben replied. "I have the Master."

They stopped at the base of the granite rock face that stretched over twenty feet wide.

"Bring 'em both over there," Ben commanded. "Lay 'em next to the crack in the center."

Buck stepped up on the granite ledge with the other little girl and carried her to the middle. Her legs and arms were tied together, so she couldn't move. Her body was shaking as she trembled with fear. Buck laid her down on the cold rock and then stepped away from her.

Wade looked down at the tiny face, her eyes pleading with him. "God forgive me," he cried, then he too stepped up onto the rock face and slowly made his way to the center next to the crack.

"Hurry it up, Wildes," Ben called, pulling out a double-sided dagger with a pentagram carved into the side. "The Master is thirsty."

Wade gently laid the little girl next to her sister, close enough to they were touching each other. He shook his head, then he turned to Ben. "We can't do this," he cried. "We can't kill these little girls."

"I'll tell you who we can…" Ben stopped and glared at Wade. "What did you do to them?"

"What?" Wade asked, turning and seeing that both children were gone. He turned back to see Ben rushing at him, a dagger drawn.

"I didn't…" he began, raising his arms defensively to protect himself from the blow. But before

348

Ben could strike, a surge of power knocked them both onto their knees, and the dagger flew from Ben's hand, clattering against the rock as it slid away.

Wade pushed himself away from Ben and crawled toward the edge of the rock. But Ben went after him, grabbing him by the ankle and pulling him back. "What did you do with them?" Ben screamed. "Give them back to me!"

"They're not here anymore."

Ben released Wade's foot and turned in astonishment to see Agnes stepping up onto the rock and looking down at him. "The girls are gone, Ben," she said. "They're safe."

"Why you!" Ben pulled back his arm to attack, but with a quick snap of her hand, Agnes sent him soaring across the rock face and crashing into the edge.

"This seems so familiar to me," Agnes said easily as she walked towards him again. "But this time, you have killed innocents. So, there is no an harm in none. Your life is forfeited."

349

Panting, Ben pushed himself up and faced her. "Bitch," he screamed. "You're no match for me…"

Agnes snapped her hand again, and Ben was thrown against the granite surface. "I'm sorry," she said, holding her head to one side. "Did you say, witch?"

Ben lay still and closed his eyes, accessing the power the Master had promised him. He could feel the cold hate running through his veins, he could feel the power harden his heart. He opened his eyes, and they were glowing blood red. Finally, he turned, waving his arm as he moved. His power shooting out.

"Mom, look out," Cat screamed.

"Bacainn!" Dustin exclaimed, creating a barrier, so the stream of energy rebounded back towards Ben and sizzled as it hit the granite.

At the edge of the granite rock face, Neal turned to his nephew. "We need to get the hell out of here," he said, turning to run toward the car.

"Yeah, we do," Buck agreed, turning around with his uncle.

"Sorry, you're going to have to stick around for a while," Henry said, standing with his hands outstretched and a ball of energy floating between them. He looked at Buck. "I remember the last time we met; I wouldn't mind giving you the same treatment."

Buck dropped to his knees and put his hands on the top of his head. "I give up," he whimpered. "Please don't hurt me."

Neal looked at Buck, and his eyes widened as Rowan and Donovan stepped out of the shadows. "We're just here to hold his beer," Donovan said. "He's got enough anger for all of us combined."

Neal looked over at Henry and followed Buck's example by dropping to his knees too.

Rowan handed Donovan two pairs of heavy iron handcuffs. "Cuff 'em, Danno. I mean, Donno," she teased. "I've always wanted to say something like that."

Donovan rolled his eyes, took the cuffs, and handcuffed each man, intertwining the chains, so they were cuffed together.

Wanda jumped up onto the granite and ran towards her father. Wade looked up and nodded, tears in his eyes. "Thank you," he sobbed. "Thank you for saving those little girls."

"Why didn't you save them, Daddy?" she asked. "Why didn't you do it yourself?"

He looked down at the ground and shook his head. "I've never been a courageous man, Wanda," he said. "I'm just not that strong."

Finias came over to them and offered his hand to Wade to help him to his feet. "I heard what you were trying to do," Finias said. "I'll make sure that's mentioned to the judge when they sentence you."

Wade nodded. "Thank you," he said. "But it wasn't nearly enough."

They walked to where Seamus, Dustin, and Agnes were standing watch over Ben. When Seamus stepped aside to let Finias through, Ben saw Wanda at his side.

"You!" he screamed. "You did this! You betrayed us!"

Wanda met his eyes and nodded. "Yeah, I did," she said. "And I'd do it again."

Seamus and Dustin pulled Ben to his feet and started to move him off the rock face when he suddenly screamed with rage and looked over his shoulder to where the dagger had fallen.

Instantly the dagger was shooting through the air toward Wanda.

"No!" Wade screamed, throwing himself in front of his daughter.

The impact of the blade threw Wade back against Wanda, and they both collapsed onto the granite. Wanda struggled up and looked down at her father, the dagger protruding from the middle of his chest. "Daddy," she cried, wrapping her arms around him. "No. No. Daddy."

Wade looked up at her and smiled. "I love you, sugar," he gasped. "Proud of you."

Then he closed his eyes and lay still in her arms.

His blood dripped from the wound in his chest onto the rock face and then spilled down the crack in the center of the rock. The granite trembled and shook, the crack suddenly glowing red.

"What's happening?" Wanda cried.

Molten rock seeped up from the crack and covered the blood, like a creature eagerly devouring its food. Then it stopped and pulled back, repulsed by the taste. It levitated, like a snake charmer's snake and slowly moved around the granite.

Ben shook his head. "It wasn't my fault," he screamed, pulling away from Seamus and Dustin. "It wasn't my fault. Wade ruined it all. It was Wade!"

The lava spewed into the air, then arced, covering Ben with fire and brimstone. He was gone before he could scream.

An hour later, Joseph and Hazel pulled up at the campgrounds, in his service vehicle, carrying two tired little girls in their arms. The parents of the twins wept in gratitude as they passed them over.

"We found them near the lake," Joseph said. "They were tired, but they seem fine."

"How can we ever thank you?" the mother asked.

"No thanks necessary, ma'am," Joseph replied. "Just doing my job."

Hazel wrapped her arm around Joseph's as they walked back to his car. "See, that wasn't a lie," she said. "We did find them by the lake."

"You're sure they will never remember any of this?" he asked.

"Cat took all of their memories of today and replaced them with a long hike in the woods," she said. "And then Rowan and Henry took away any aches and pains they may have suffered."

"We won today," Joseph said, heaving a sigh of relief.

Hazel nodded. "Yes, we did," she said. "And we're going to win tomorrow, too!"

Chapter Fifty-two

Wanda slipped out of Agnes' Jeep without saying a word and made her way across the driveway to her car.

"Wait, Wanda," Agnes called, running over to her. "What are you doing?"

Wanda took a deep breath to push back the tears and waited a moment to speak, so her voice wouldn't tremble. She tried to smile but ended up just biting back more tears. "I'm going home," she said. "You know, my apartment, I'll be safe there now."

"No," Agnes said.

Wanda was confused. "What? I'll be safe," she argued. "Ben's gone."

Agnes put her arm around the young woman's shoulders and turned her away from her car. "No, you're not going home," she said. "You're going to stay here with us tonight. You need family."

Wanda resisted. "I'm sorry, but you're not my family," she said sadly. "My only family died tonight on the rock."

Tears filled her eyes and spilled over, trailing down her cheeks. Agnes sighed and wrapped her arms around Wanda, hugging her. Wanda stiffened for a moment, but suddenly, it was as if her emotional dam collapsed, and she put her head on Agnes' shoulder and sobbed. Agnes just held her, rubbing her back and whispering soft words of comfort.

"He…he did love me," Wanda sobbed.

"Yes, he did," Agnes replied. "Enough to save your life."

Wanda's breath came out in small gasps. "He was brave," she agreed.

"So brave," Agnes soothed. "And I believe he would have saved those little girls if we hadn't come along."

Wanda nodded, and more tears streamed down her face.

"And he was so proud of you," Agnes added. "He was so happy to see what you had done."

"I made him proud tonight," she cried. "I don't know if that ever happened before."

"Oh, I'm sure it did," Agnes said. "But I don't think he knew how to express his feelings."

Wanda sniffled and lifted her head to meet Agnes' eyes. "I loved him," she said, her lips quivering with emotion, and her eyes swollen with tears. "I really did love him."

"I know," Agnes said. "And he really loved you too. And he loved your mother, so much. I remember seeing him at her funeral, he was devastated. The two of you were everything to him."

Taking a deep, shaking breath, Wanda wiped away some of the tears on her face and nodded. "Thank you," she said. "Thank you for opening your home to me. Thank you for letting me be part of your family today. I'll never forget it."

She started to step away, but Agnes stopped her.

359

"I'm sorry," Agnes said. "But you are not going home. You need family, and whether you like it or not, you are now part of our family." She smiled tenderly at Wanda. "Cousin Wanda."

A soggy chuckle escaped Wanda's lips, but she shook her head. "Thank you, but no, really," she said. "I can't…"

"I thought you promised to help with the handfasting," Agnes reminded her.

Wanda's eyes widened in astonishment. "You really want me to be here?" she asked, confused.

Agnes nodded and then met Wanda's eyes, so she could see the truth in them. "I, we, really want you to be here," she said. "I don't know what tomorrow is going to bring. But I would be honored to have you on our side of it."

"My mom would have wanted me to help," Wanda said softly, then she smiled. "And, actually, my dad would have too."

Joseph's car pulled up in the driveway behind them, and Hazel opened her door and stood up. "Hey, everyone," she called out. "We brought food! Pizza!!"

Then she turned to Wanda. "What's your favorite kind?"

Wanda dashed away the remaining tears and smiled. "Pepperoni and mushroom, extra cheese," she replied.

Hazel grinned widely. "Dang, girl, we are related!" she laughed.

Agnes slipped her arm through Wanda's and turned her back toward the house, chuckling softly. "I guess that's that," she said.

Wanda laughed and nodded. "I guess so."

Chapter Fifty-three

Agnes woke up the next morning with the smell of bacon wafting in the air, and Fuzzy nudging her to open the bedroom door.

"Just a minute," she chided the giant wolf who kept leaning against her to herd her towards the door. "I have to at least put a robe on."

Fuzzy whined softly.

"You're not going to starve in the time it takes me to grab my robe," she said, rolling her eyes. "Get a grip, it's only bacon."

Fuzzy sent her a look that would have chilled the hearts of lesser women, and she laughed. "Okay, I realize how important bacon is in your life," she apologized, reaching for the doorknob. She opened her door and Fuzzy bounded out.

"Really, no need to wait for me," she said softly to the retreating canine. "I can find my own way."

She padded across the great room and into the kitchen to be met by more wondrous smells of breakfast, blueberry pancakes, hot maple syrup, bacon and sausages, and fresh orange juice. And in the middle of it all was Seamus singing and doing a little jig as he flipped pancakes.

"You're getting married in the morning," he sang. "Ding, dong, the bells are going to chime."

"Seamus?" Agnes asked, startling him. "What is all this?"

"Agnes, darling, light of my life," he said, as he tossed Fuzzy a piece of bacon. "And don't you look like the rarest of flowers on your wedding day."

She ran her hand through her hair, realizing that the only flower she might be resembling at that moment would have been a storm-tossed chrysanthemum and smiled. "Why thank you," she said, slipping onto a stool near the counter and picking up a piece of bacon. "But what's going on?"

"This is an official wedding breakfast," he said. "Generally, it's served after the wedding, but since the ceremony's going to be a wee bit late, I thought we'd start the day on the right foot."

She looked at the platters piled high with food. "Are we expecting an army to join us?" she asked.

He laughed loudly. "No, but we've got a bunch of fine strapping laddies," he replied. "I'm sure they'll finish this up and be asking for more."

She bit into the crisp bacon and sighed softly. It was perfectly done, something she could rarely do. "Do I have time to shower before we eat?" she asked.

He nodded. "Darling, it's your day, too," he said kindly. "You take all the time you need, but breakfast will be served in ten minutes."

She jumped up and popped the rest of the bacon in her mouth. "I'll be back in eight!"

As she was leaving the kitchen, a bed-rumpled Hazel was coming down the stairs, her nose in the air sniffing softly. "I thought I was dreaming at first," she said yawning. "But even dreams don't smell this good."

"Have a seat, young lady," Seamus said. "Since you're eating for two, I don't think it would hurt for you to have a wee head start on the others."

Hazel walked over and kissed him on the cheek. "You're my hero," she said with a smile.

"Hey," Joseph teased as he walked into the kitchen through the back door. "I'm gone for a few hours, and you're kissing another man."

Hazel grinned at him. "He made me breakfast, with bacon," she replied. "And sausage."

Joseph, and his six-foot, five-inch frame, walked across the room and stood next to the diminutive Irish man. "Bacon and sausage?" he asked, his eyebrow arching in mock surprise. "I might have to kiss him myself."

Seamus chuckled and shook his head. "Well, not wishing to offend," he teased, his eyes sparkling with mirth. "But I never could abide being kissed by someone with a moustache and beard. There was once this wee lass from the circus…"

Joseph shook his head. "I don't think I want to hear this," he said.

Seamus winked at them. "Aye, that's just what she said when I had to turn her down," he replied with a grin. "Do you have time for breakfast?"

"If you don't mind, I'll take some with me," he said, and then the turned to Hazel. "I have to go to the station and make sure Neal and Buck are transferred to the prison guards that are coming for them. I shouldn't be very long."

She smiled up at him with such love that Seamus' heart melted a little. "Don't be too long," she said, reaching up and kissing him. "We have a big day today."

He hugged her to him. "A big day?" he asked, acting confused. "A big day." He pondered that for a moment, and then he nodded. "That's right, it's stall cleaning day for the goats."

She punched him softly in the stomach and wrinkled up her nose. "You keep that up, and you'll be sleeping with the goats tonight," she said.

He bent down and kissed her passionately. "I'll be back as soon as I can," he said, his voice thick with emotion.

She nodded and placed her hand on his chest. "Hurry home," she whispered.

Seamus filled a plate for Hazel and waited until the door closed behind Joseph to put it on the counter in front of her. "It's a shame the two of you don't get along at all," he teased.

She laughed and nodded. "Yeah, it's something that we're going to have to work on."

Chapter Fifty-four

Finias, Dustin, and Seamus sat on the front porch of the Willoughby house, away from the rest of the family.

"Any more dreams?" Seamus asked Finias.

"The same one," Finias replied. "But, no new answers."

"So, how do we handle the fight tonight?" Dustin asked.

The front door opened, and Agnes slipped outside. "I believe I need to be a part of this conversation," she said. "And we're going to have to bring the others in at some point."

Finias sighed and nodded. "You're right," he said. "But try as we might, we can't see anything clearly."

Agnes sat down near them and nodded. "In my dream, I'm in the cave," she said. "Last night, I saw that you three were down there with me, in the quaternary knot. And we were fighting the demon from there. Then I was running somewhere in the dark, and I could see the gravestones from the Willoughby cemetery."

"My dream was similar," Dustin said with a nod.

"As was mine," Seamus added. "So, are we agreeing that the cemetery means we're not going to make it?"

Finias shook his head. "I didn't feel dead," he argued. "I felt like I was still fighting."

Agnes nodded. "Well, perhaps we were," she speculated. "Our spirits could still fight. As a matter of fact, they'd be less encumbered because we wouldn't be worried about dying."

"She has a point," Seamus said. "But whatever happens, we've all seen it in our dreams, and there's no turning back at this point. Agreed?"

"Agreed," Dustin and Finias replied.

"But we need to be sure the others don't know about this part of it," Agnes said. "They need to concentrate on the demon from the granite face access point. If they're worried about us dying, they won't be able to save themselves."

"You're right," Finias agreed. "So, let's meet with them and let them know that we've had corresponding dreams that tell us that we four need to be inside the cave before midnight, and they need to be on the surface."

"I have one more request," Agnes said, looking at the men surrounding her. She felt blessed that they had all become an essential part of their family in such a short time. And grateful that they were all willing to sacrifice themselves to save her daughters. "First, I want you all to know how grateful I am for your willingness to be here, to sacrifice for us. This wasn't part of the agreement when I first met you, but I know that we wouldn't have come this far without your help."

"It wasn't part of the agreement, no," Seamus said. "But these past few weeks have brought me more joy than I could have imagined. So, there's no debt owed."

Dustin nodded. "I'm honored to be part of this," he said. "And I'm so grateful for the job you've done raising our daughters. They are such amazing people."

Finias reached over and took her hand in his. "This is where I am meant to be," he said.

She dashed a tear from her cheek and smiled at them. "Thank you," she said. "And now, my request. As you, each of you, participate in the handfasting ceremonies for your daughters. Will you please remember to bless them with long lives and joy? Words are powerful. Blessings are powerful. And we can use all the help we can get."

Chapter Fifty-five

"So, what do you think?" Rowan asked Henry as they sat in the Still Room searching through the grimoire Henry's ancestor had left them.

Henry looked up at her, his eyes filled with despair. "I'm sorry," he said. "I can't find anything to help us."

Rowan sat back in her chair and covered her face with her hands. Then she dropped her hands, looked over at him, and shook her head. "No!" she exclaimed angrily. "No! I will not have worked this far and done so much to just give up. There has to be a way. It cannot end like this."

Henry got out of his chair and knelt before her, taking her hands in his own. "I didn't mean there wasn't hope," he said, lifting one of her hands to his lips. "There's always hope. What I meant, and what's so hard for me to accept, is the way isn't clear. I don't have the answers. I can't figure it out."

Rowan placed her hand on the side of Henry's head and gently combed through his hair. "Ah, I see," she said. "You want an analytical assessment of all of the parameters in the situation and the varying degrees of success in each hypothetical perambulation."

He shrugged, slightly embarrassed, and nodded. "Is that too much to ask for?" he asked quietly.

She leaned down and kissed him, her heart swelling with love. She couldn't imagine her life without this brilliant, brave, and slightly self-conscious man. She simply adored him. "No, it's not too much to ask for," she whispered, her face only inches from his. "But, once again, I think we're asked to walk in faith."

He sighed. "Faith is so…"

"Unknown?" she prompted.

"Risky," he replied, lifting his hand to cradle her face. "I can't risk you getting hurt. My life would end…"

She placed her hand over his mouth and shook her head. "Faith is the only thing we can rely on," she said. "It's our only reasonable option. We know love lasts

373

forever; we've seen it through Patience and the Willoughby sisters. No matter what happens tonight, I will love you forever."

He reached up and kissed her tenderly, gliding his thumb along her cheek. "I don't think forever is going to be long enough," he whispered.

She smiled at him. "Okay, well, let's just start with forever, and then we can take it from there."

Chapter Fifty-six

The sky was nearly cloudless, and the sun warmed their backs as Cat and Donovan walked up the ridge to the small cave where they'd first met. They held hands but didn't say a word, both lost in their own thoughts as they reached the top of the escarpment. A cool autumn breeze rattled the gold and red leaves on the maple trees below them and a bald-eagle glided above them, soaring in the sky.

They finally reached the shelter, partially hidden by brush, and silently entered it. The temperature of the air dropped immediately when they stepped out of the sun, into the cave, and Cat shivered. Donovan shrugged off his jacket and placed it over her shoulders.

She smiled up at him. "You used to do this all the time," she said, her voice tight with emotion.

He shook his head. "You never could remember to bring a sweater," he replied with a teasing smile.

She lifted the collar of the jacket to her nose and inhaled. "That's because I loved to have your scent surrounding me," she replied and inhaled again. "Strong, sexy man."

"I see," he said, wrapped his arms around her waist and pulling her closer. "It was a plot."

She nodded. "A well-crafted plot," she replied.

"But what you don't know is that when you wore it, your scent would rub off on my jacket," he said. "And I would bring it to bed with me, dreaming that you were in my arms."

She shivered again, but this time it wasn't from the cold. She laid her head against his shoulder and wrapped her arms around his waist. "I wish I would have known," she whispered.

He kissed her head and smiled. "Why? Would you have come to me and laid in my arms?"

She smiled and shook her head. "No, I would have sent you a bottle of my favorite perfume."

She could feel his laughter rumble in his chest and sighed.

"It wasn't just the perfume," he whispered, bending over and kissing her neck.

"No?" she breathed. "What was it?"

"It was the scent of your skin, spicy and sweet," he said, pressing another kiss on her neck. "It was the scent of your breath, as you sighed." Then he gently lifted her chin with his hand so he could see her eyes. "And it was the taste of your mouth under mine."

He slowly lowered his lips to hers and tasted, tenderly and softly at first. Then, when she moaned with desire, he crushed his lips against hers and feasted on her taste. She slipped her hands up his back, along his neck, and then through his hair, pulling him closer. Taking as well as giving.

Slowly, he gentled the kiss, and finally, after one last lingering touch, he lifted his head and met her eyes.

"It has always been you, Cat," he said. "From the moment I first laid eyes on you, I was enchanted."

"You have always been my knight in shining armor," she said. "I would dream of you, even when I thought there was no hope. I have always loved you."

He stepped back, and they linked hands. "When I think of how much time I wasted…"

She shook her head. "No, don't," she interrupted. "No regrets. No rehashing the past. We have the future, and whatever that future holds, I'm so grateful you'll be there with me."

He lifted her hand and brought it to his lips. "I want three children," he murmured as he pressed another kiss on her skin.

"What?" she asked, surprised.

He smiled at her. "I just thought I ought to let you know my intentions," he said, his eyes filled with love. "I'd like three children. All girls."

She smiled at him, a saucy smile. "Well, since I've never done this before," she said. "I'm afraid I'm going to need lots of practice."

"Raising children?" he asked.

She smiled and shook her head. "No, making them."

He looked down at her, his eyes filled with desire, and pressed an opened-mouthed kiss on her palm. She shivered at the intimacy of both the look in his eye and the touch of his mouth on her sensitive skin. "It will be my pleasure," he whispered. "My very great pleasure."

Chapter Fifty-seven

They met together in the afternoon, each couple with their own mixture of anticipation and fear as they approached the evening. They stood around the table, the meeting feeling more formal than their usual family get-togethers. Agnes looked around the table at the faces of all the people she loved and wondered if she would ever have an opportunity to meet with them again, like this. She prayed that she would.

"Blessed be," Agnes said softly, as she began the meeting.

"Blessed be," they all replied.

"Please sit down," she requested, slipping into her own seat.

She waited until they were all seated, then she began. "Today is a day we've anticipated for a long time," she said. "And not too long ago, we were advised to seek for joy on this day, not to worry about things beyond our control. So, I want to make this meeting brief, so we can get on with the preparations for the handfasting."

She took a deep breath and continued. "Over the past few days, I've had a dream about tonight. And as we all know, dreams or visions about ourselves can often be incomplete or incorrect," she said. "But, as I've spoken with Finias, Dustin, and Seamus, they have all had similar dreams. Dreams that perhaps offered a strategy for this evening."

"You've all dreamt this?" Cat asked.

Agnes nodded. "Yes," she said. "And the dreams are surprisingly alike. In the dream, Finias, Seamus, Dustin, and I are in the cave where the spell was first cast."

"But there was a cave-in down there," Henry said. "There is no cave left."

"Well, as a matter of fact," Dustin interjected. "Several nights ago, Finias led Seamus and me out to the cave. I was able to clean out the debris and also add some structural supports to keep it safe."

Hazel smiled at him. "Way to go, Dad," she said.

"We cleared away the dust from the floor," Finias added. "And the etching of the quaternary knot is still down there."

"Okay," Donovan said. "So, if you four are down below, how do we handle the circle up above?"

"Well, since Patience was my ancestor," Henry suggested. "I could take the fourth spot."

Cat shook her head and smiled at her mom. "Well, suddenly, it all makes sense," she said.

"What?" Agnes asked.

"I kept meditating on tonight, trying to figure out what we were supposed to do," Cat replied. "And I kept seeing the white room, where the other spell was cast. But I couldn't figure out why. Why is that image important?"

She turned to Wanda. "It's because we need you," she said. "You should be the fourth. You should be there to use your power to reverse what your ancestor did."

As soon as Cat issued the invitation, Wanda knew it was right. She knew that her mother would want her there, alongside the Willoughbys, to fight against the demon. "I'd be honored," she said. "It feels right, doesn't it?"

"Yes, it does," Agnes agreed, and then she stood up. "And now, since we know how things will proceed later tonight, we need to prepare for the joyful part of the day. Men, you are all hereby tossed out of the house while we women get ready for this evening."

Joseph shrugged. "Sounds like time for a bachelor party, right?"

Finias nodded. "Yes, why don't we all meet outside in a few minutes and plan from there?"

"Great," Henry said. "Let's go."

The men left the room, and the women looked at each other. "Bachelor party?" Hazel asked skeptically.

"You know they're going to the cave," Cat said.

"Oh!" Agnes said, hurrying from the table. "I almost forgot."

She ran through the house to the back door.

"I didn't want the women to worry," Finias said, standing with the men on the ground below the back porch, "but I think we should go back to the cave once more."

Joseph nodded. "I was thinking the same thing," he agreed. "I'd like to plot things out in the light of day."

"Do you think they'll figure it out?" Dustin asked.

Agnes pushed open the back door and stepped outside.

The men stopped talking and looked up at her. She caught her breath and smiled at them. "When you're at the cave," she said, "could you please etch another quaternary knot on the rock face above? Thanks so much."

Then she turned around and went back into the house.

"How did she…" Henry asked.

Finias just smiled and shook his head. "Gentlemen, these are very dangerous women we are associated with."

Donovan chuckled. "And we wouldn't have it any other way."

Chapter Fifty-eight

A soft breeze danced across the grass, carrying with it the scent of the autumn leaves, the moist earth, the spicy fragrance of fall foliage, and the mystical scent of wax candles. The circle of oaks, their trunks thick and straight, stood as sentinels guarding the old ways, the sacred rites performed within their shadows. Their uppermost limbs, still decorated with golden leaves, were intertwined, forming an arched dome, a cathedral of nature to perform the handfast.

Henry, Joseph, Donovan, and Finias stood at one end of the circle, each dressed in their own version of formalwear.

Finias wore a multi-colored turban on his head and a matching robe with a gold braided band around his waist. His chest was bare, and he wore dark harem pants that tied several inches above his bare feet.

Henry wore a traditional English Morning Suit, the suitcoat with tails was black, the vest was dove gray, and the slacks were black and gray pinstripe. His ascot was silver, and the tiepin was a family heirloom of rainbow opal.

The Wulffolk traditional wedding attire that Joseph wore consisted of light tan deerskin lederhosen with green and blue embroidery. His white linen shirt with full sleeves was also embroidered on the sleeve. The long wool vest was sky blue with gold buttons and fitted tightly across his chest. His knee-high wool socks matched the vest and his leather boots gleamed with a high sheen.

Donovan wore a slim-fitting tuxedo in black with a gray striped shirt and a white embroidered cummerbund that matched the corset from Cat's dress.

To each side of the men, tall candlesticks holding thick pillar candles glowed in the night. Below the candlesticks were copper urns overflowing with white roses, white lilies, white hydrangeas, and baby's breath. A thousand tiny lights sparkled in the trees, and a sliver of the moon shone down from its apex in the night sky.

White tulle was draped between the trees and vines of English ivy curled around it.

Suddenly a light appeared beyond the circle, and it drew the attention of all the men. The light grew in size as it approached, and they could see it was a large lantern held on the end of a pole. Seamus walked up through the narrow pathway, the pole in his hands, lighting the way for the rest of the procession.

He entered the circle, walked to the side, and slid the end of the pole into the ground.

Wanda, dressed in a long silver gown, entered next, tossing white rose petals from a large basket she carried. She walked the entire circumference of the circle, so all the grass was scattered with the delicate petals. Then she stepped back to wait on the edge of the circle.

Dustin entered next, carrying another lantern. He went across the circle, opposite Seamus, and slid the pole into the ground. Then turned to look back at the pathway.

Hazel entered first, her hair flowing over her shoulders adorned with a crown of white roses. She was holding a simple bouquet also of white roses. She walked slowly into the circle and made her way to stand several feet in front of Joseph.

"You look perfect," he whispered in awe.

She smiled, her love shining from her eyes. "So, do you," she whispered back.

Rowan entered next, and Henry's quick intake of breath echoed in the circle. Her hair was swept up in a loose bun and a satin ribbon and baby's breath were woven throughout. She carried a bouquet of lavender and baby's breath with white ribbons streaming from it. She walked across the circle and then stood in line with Hazel and across from Henry.

Henry stared at her with such intensity she blushed. "Do you like it?" she whispered.

"I didn't think I could fall more in love with you," he replied softly. "I was wrong."

Cat entered next, her curls flowing free with two lilies holding back her hair on one side. Her bouquet was filled with long-stemmed lilies, feathery ferns, and several birds of paradise for color. Her head held high, she walked with stately grace to step in line with her sisters and meet Donovan's eyes.

"You are simply magnificent," he said, his eyes filled with admiration.

She smiled at him, her heart pounding in her chest. "I love you," she whispered back.

Finally, Agnes entered the circle. Her gown was ivory lace with a fitted bodice and long lace sleeves. It had a V-shaped waistline and a full satin skirt with lace embroidery with a long laced-covered train. She had decided to forgo her veil and follow her daughters' styles with her hair pulled back in a low bun with a cluster of roses and baby's breath above it. She carried one single white rose in her hands.

Finias stepped from his place, met her in the center of the circle, and lifted her hand to his lips. "I couldn't wait," he whispered.

She smiled up at him and nodded. "I'm glad," she replied.

He led her to her place in line and then went back to his place.

"And now we'll begin the ceremony," Seamus announced.

Chapter Fifty-nine

Wanda came forward with her basket and pulled out four long lengths of satin-covered cord.

"Please step towards each other and clasp hands," Seamus requested.

The couples moved together and clasped their hand on the arm of their partner, above the other's wrist, so their pulses beat together.

Dustin took a cord from Wanda and made a loop in the middle of it and laid it over Hazel and Joseph's hands, with the loop hanging down on one side and the loose ends hanging over the other. He picked up the loose ends and tied them together in a loose knot, then he slipped the knot underneath their hands and slid it through the loop.

He placed his hand over the cord on the top of their clasped hands. Then he looked at each of them with pride and love. "Hazel and Joseph, by this cord, you are bound to your vows. With his knot, your lives are bound together. You have already learned the strength of two combined, sharing the best parts of each, and supporting one another. You have witnessed the miracle and the joy of two creating three. Another life still bound by a cord within Hazel's womb. With the entwining of this knot, you start your family. You create a legacy that will last for the eternities. A legacy of love, long life, happiness, and peace."

Hazel took a deep breath and met Joseph's eyes. "As this knot is tied, so I bind my heart to yours," Hazel said. "I bind with it my love, my laughter, my dreams, my hopes, and my fears. All I am is yours, for now, and for forever."

Joseph stared down at her for a long moment, his heart too full to speak. He finally cleared his throat and took a deep breath. "My beloved Hazel," he began. "As this knot is tied, so I bind my heart to yours. My heart has been yours since the moment we met. My life has been yours since you saved it with your own. My love has been yours since the beginning of time. You are my own love, my eternal companion, my one and only, forever."

Dustin squeezed their hands in a show of affection, then lifted his hand from theirs and stepped back. "Let the knot be tied," he said. "With the tying of the knot, the vow is made. Joseph and Hazel are husband and wife."

The couple slipped their hands backwards, catching on to the cord as they did so, and tying a knot in the cord as they pulled away. Then Joseph caught Hazel up in his arms and kissed her, twirling her around in a circle. "You are mine forever," he said.

She kissed him back. "And you are mine," she said. "And don't you forget it."

He laughed and shook his head. "Never," he said. "I will never forget it."

He put her on the ground and, with his arm around her waist, pulled her next to him so they could watch the next ceremony.

Seamus took a cord from Wanda and made a loop in the middle of it. He laid it over Rowan and Henry's clasped hands. "Your turn now," he said and smiled at them. "Let's see if I can remember how to do this. I'm not an engineer like Dustin."

He threaded the ends through the loop and made a loose knot at the end.

"That seems to have done the trick," he said, winking at Rowan. "Now comes the serious part."

Then he placed his hand over their hands, and his voice now filled with sincerity.

"As this knot is tied, so are your lives now bound," he explained. "Woven into this cord are your dreams, your vows, your love, and the inseparable strength you share as a couple. Two now become one, stronger by the combining. With the entwining of this knot, you tie all the desires, dreams, love, long life, and happiness wished here in this place to your lives for as long as love shall last."

Rowan looked up at Henry. "As this knot is tied, so I bind my heart to yours," she said. "Through this life and through eternity, through light and dark, through happiness and sorrow, we shall always be together."

Henry looked into Rowan's eyes and saw her love for him shining there. He knew that he was the luckiest man in the world. "As this knot is tied, so I bind my heart to yours," he said. "Through this life and through eternity, I will be there to love you, protect you, cherish you, and put you before all others."

Seamus lifted his hand from theirs and stepped back. "Let the knot be tied," he said. "With the tying of the knot, the vow is made. Henry and Rowan are husband and wife."

Rowan and Henry slipped their hands backwards, catching on to the cord as they did so, and tying a knot in the cord as they pulled away.

Then Henry leaned over and kissed Rowan, holding her close. "I love you," he whispered.

"I love you back," she sighed and kissed him again.

They stepped back, arm in arm, and watch Finias step out of line and pick up a cord from Wanda. He made a loop in it and laid it over Cat and Donovan's hands. Then, following the same pattern as the others, he knotted the ends and slipped the knot through the loop.

He placed his hand over the cord and smiled at Cat. "You look so beautiful, my daughter," he said. "I am honored to be here, this day, with the man you love."

Then he turned to Donovan. "The greatest compliment I can offer you is that I trust you with her heart," he said.

Donovan nodded. "Thank you," he said, his voice hoarse with emotion.

Finias took a deep breath and began, "Two entwined as one, as the cord becomes a knot, bound by commitment, honor, love, and faith. As this knot is tied, so your lives are now bound together for this life and the next. Together you grow, together you learn, together you experience life – the pain and the joy, the happiness, and the sorrow, the good and the bad. Remember, together you can conquer anything. As this knot is tied, I bless you with a long life, happiness, and an overabundance of love."

Cat smiled up at Donovan, her heart filled with love. "Donovan, as this knot is tied, so I bind my heart to yours," she said. "But even without the knot, my heart has always been inexplicably bound to yours. You are my soulmate. You are the one person who understands me better than I understand myself. With you in my life, I am finally whole. I will love you for eternity."

Donovan leaned over their clasped hands and gently kissed Cat's lips. Then he straightened and met her eyes. "Catalpa, as this knot is tied, so I bind my heart to yours," he said. "You saved me. You believed in me when no one else would. You saw something worthy in me that no one else saw. Your faith has made me who I am today. And your love makes me want to be a better man each and every day. I love you, for now, and for eternity."

Finias lifted his hand from theirs and stepped back. "Let the knot be tied," he said. "With the tying of the knot, the vow is made. Donovan and Catalpa are husband and wife."

Catalpa and Donovan slipped their hands backwards, catching on to the cord as they did so, and tying a knot in the cord as they pulled away.

Donovan cradled Cat's head in his hand and kissed her deeply, pouring all of his love into the kiss. Cat wrapped her arms around his neck, kissing him back with all the joy she was feeling in her heart. Finally, he stepped back, leaning forward once more for a tender kiss, and then he drew her into his arms, to watch the final ceremony.

Chapter Sixty

Finias stepped back in place, across from Agnes, and waited. Each of the daughters turned and kissed their new husbands, then stepped away from them and hurried over to Wanda. From the basket, each of them pulled a long satin ribbon and carried them over to Finias and Agnes.

Cat made a loop with her blue one first and laid it over their hands. Rowan made a loop of her green one next and placed it on top of Cat's ribbon. Then Hazel made a loop with her gold one and placed it over the other two.

Hazel bent down and lifted up the ends of all three ribbons and tied them into one loose knot and slipped it through the three loops made by the ribbons. Then all three girls placed their hands over the ribbons and the couple's hands.

"As this knot is tied, so are your lives now bound," Cat said. "Not bound with words, not bound with promises, but bound with love."

"As this knot is tied, so are your lives now bound," Rowan repeated. "Bound with endless joy, bound with new adventures, and bound with honor and respect."

"As this knot is tied, so are your lives now bound," Hazel said. "Bound together so you can take care of each other, not bound to responsibilities or worries, but bound for a journey through the eternities as husband and wife."

Agnes looked up at Finias. "As this knot is tied, so I bind my heart to yours," she vowed. "You have always been the love of my life. You have always been the man I'd hope to spend the eternities with, and I thought…" She paused and took a deep, shuddering breath. "I thought I lost that chance. But now that I've been given another opportunity to love you forever, I vow that I will treasure every moment I have with you, in this life and the next."

Finias lifted his other hand and cradled Agnes' face. "Agnes, my only love," he said. "As this knot is tied, so I bind my heart to yours. You touched my heart as no other ever did. Even though we were parted, I always felt a connection to you. The years may have passed, but that did not lessen my love and desire for you. You were my first love and my only true love. I look forward to our next adventures together, in this life and the next."

"That was really great," Hazel said, wiping the tears from her cheeks. "Both of you."

The sisters lifted their hands from over the ribbons and stepped back. "Let the knot be tied," Catalpa said.

"With the tying of the knot, the vow is made," Rowan added.

Finias and Mom, I mean, Agnes, are husband and wife," Hazel finished.

Agnes and Finias slipped their hands backwards, catching on to the cord as they did so, and tying a knot in the cord as they pulled away.

Finias pulled Agnes to him and kissed her, sealing their promises for all to witness. A few moments later, he broke off the kiss, tenderly kissing her on her forehead and then stepped back.

"I adore you," he said.

"And I you," she replied.

"Well, now, do we have time for a celebration?" Seamus asked.

Finias looked at his watch and shook his head. "No, unfortunately," he said. "The party will have to wait until after Samhain is over."

Chapter Sixty-one

Their wedding finery had been exchanged for black jeans, dark shirts, and sturdy hiking boots. The women had their hair pulled back, so it could not be grabbed and used against them. They stood together in a circle in the parking lot near the granite rock face; their faces were somber, but their energy was high, and their determination was solid.

"The park is shut down," Joseph explained. "I've told my men that something was going down here tonight and to keep the public out. Those who aren't coven think it's a drug bust, those who are coven will know exactly what we're dealing with."

"Are we going to have to worry about any of them joining in with the demon?" Cat asked.

Joseph shook his head. "No, they don't have a leader to rally them," he said. "So, they might be angry, but they aren't organized."

"And they really aren't very brave," Donovan added. "They would rather grumble in bars and on the internet than actually do something."

"Oh, good," Hazel said, trying to keep her voice light. "So, all we have to worry about is a demon and his legions. Good to know."

"Listen to me," Agnes said, using her mom voice. "We are going to succeed tonight. We are going to defeat the demon. We are going to triumph. We are going to fulfill the final part of our ancestors' incantation. And the reason is that we have the secret weapon – something this demon has no comprehension of – we have love. Love stopped him in the first place. Love brought us here. And love will carry us through tonight."

She stopped as tears filled her eyes and clogged her throat. She looked around at all of the people she loved standing in this circle, and her heart filled with joy. She knew that if she did not live to see them all again, they would continue to love one another and take care of each other. She shook her head, clearing it of morose thoughts, then took a deep breath and continued.

"I love you all so much. I am so proud of you, the choices you've made, the challenges you have faced to get here, and the faith you've shown by being here tonight. Catalpa, Rowan, and Hazel, you have always been the greatest blessings in my life. I just want you to know that. I'm so grateful you have found partners who not only love you, but adore you, and will do everything in their power to keep you safe. My new sons, I trust you with my daughters' hearts. That's the greatest compliment I can offer."

She took another deep breath and then lifted her wand up toward the night sky. "And now we fight," she called out, and a stream of pure blue light streamed into the darkness.

"We fight!" the others in the group called, pulling their wands out and allowing their power to stream heavenward, so the sky above the park shimmered above them with the power and majesty of the northern lights.

Agnes lowered her wand and then walked over to Cat and hugged her. "Blessed be," she whispered.

"Blessed be, Mom," Cat replied, hugging her back.

Then she walked over to Rowan and hugged her too. "Blessed be," she said.

Rowan threw her arms around her mother. "I love you," she said, then she stepped back.

Finally, Agnes walked over to Hazel. She put her hand lightly on Hazel's stomach and smiled at her daughter. "You are going to be such an amazing mother," she said, then she hugged Hazel. "Blessed be."

Hazel's eyes filled with tears, and she leaned back to meet her mother's eyes. "Mom, is everything okay?" she asked, concerned.

Agnes forced a smile and nodded. "Of course, it is," she said. "I just needed some hugs before we, how do you say it, kick some demon ass?"

Hazel chuckled and nodded. "Blessed be, Mom," she replied, kissing Agnes on the cheek. "Go kick ass!"

Agnes stepped away from her daughters and then walked over to Wanda, hugging her as well. "Blessed be," she said.

Wanda smiled. "Thank you," she said. "I've missed my mother more than you know. I felt her hug come through you."

"Our loved ones on the other side of the veil are often closer than we realize," Agnes replied.

She stepped back and joined Finias, Seamus, and Dustin.

"We'll see you on the other side," Seamus said with a smile. "And until we meet again, may God hold you in the hollow of His hand."

The four walked to Agnes' Jeep, climbed in, and drove away.

Rowan turned to Cat. "Was it my imagination, or did that sound like Seamus was saying goodbye and not in a good way?" she asked.

Cat shook her head, not wanting to admit that she'd thought the very same thing. "No, of course not," she lied. "That's just Seamus' Irish coming out."

Rowan breathed a sigh of relief. "You're right," she agreed. "Let's go get ready."

Chapter Sixty-two

Using four-wheel drive, Agnes was able to drive the Jeep to the opening of the cave. She pulled in close and started to park.

"Agnes, how much do you like your Jeep?" Dustin asked from the backseat.

"I love my Jeep," she replied.

"Then, you might want to park it a bit further away from the opening," he suggested. "Just in case there's a repeat performance of what happened in the cave last time."

She nodded slowly and put the car back into gear. "Good idea."

She parked the Jeep on the side of the cave, away from the opening, and they all climbed out. Finias put his hand on Agnes' shoulder and when she looked up to question him, he shook his head. "We don't know what our dreams meant," he said. "We can't enter that cave with the idea that we're going to all die. We need to have faith, Agnes. We need to have hope. Where there are fear and doubt, hope and faith cannot survive."

"Okay, you're right," she agreed. "It's just that I have so much to lose."

"Aye, and that's all the reason to believe you're going to win," Seamus said. "We have more at stake. We're going to fight harder." Then he smiled at Agnes. "Besides, you're quite a bit prettier than any demon I've ever seen and that's got to count for something."

Agnes smiled and then laughed. "And you are much more charming than anyone has the right to be," she replied. "Thank you. I'm ready to win."

They walked to the entrance of the cave, pulled their wands out to light their way, and proceeded down the path that led the way to the chamber. Agnes could see the new steel beams supporting the walls and the ceiling of the cave. She turned to Dustin and smiled. "Nice job on the supports," she said.

"Well, let's just see if they can withstand fire and brimstone," he replied. "If they do, I'm going to be using them in a couple of projects in Colorado."

She chuckled and nodded. "I can just see it on the specifications, tested for use in fire and brimstone environments."

Dustin shook his head. "No, I'd say something like tested for thermomechanical fatigue in elevated temperature environments."

"Wow, impressive," Agnes replied.

Dustin grinned. "And that's why they pay me the big bucks," he teased.

They stopped at the entrance of the chamber, and Agnes gasped softly. The quaternary knot surrounded a large pit of gently boiling, putrid molten rock. "I should have brought air freshener," she said, waving her hand over her face.

"Oh, I can help with that," Seamus said, and he waved his wand. Suddenly the room was filled with the fragrance of a clover field. "Just bringing a wee bit of home with me."

Agnes stepped inside and looked around, then she stopped and stared at the walls. "Did you see that?" she asked.

Finias turned to look at where she was pointing. "What?" he asked.

She used her wand to illuminate the darkened shadows near the cave walls, and suddenly they could all see their reflections.

"I wonder if the lava filled this chamber and superheated the walls," Dustin mused. "Which would cause the silica in the rock to turn to glass and be able to reflect our images."

"It's a mirror chamber," Seamus said, looking around at the images of them being reflected back and forth, over and over again. "We go on forever, don't we?"

"I like that we have an army of us," Agnes said, taking her place in the knot. "And now it's time to put the army to use."

The three men took their places in the knot, and they all pointed their wands toward the pit. Agnes nodded to each of the men and then cast her spell.

"Three and one to seal the pit,

Parents, guardians, warriors we,

Three and one to end the curse,

As we ask, so mote it be.

Suddenly the lava flamed to life, bubbling over the edges and seeping toward the four.

"Now, we fight!" Finias yelled.

Chapter Sixty-three

The other part of the group moved quietly and swiftly through the woods toward the bluff above the lake. The moon was only a thin sliver in the night sky, and thousands of stars glittered overhead. A cool breeze whistled through the trees bringing with it the contrasting odor of sulfur.

"We're getting closer," Cat said. "I can smell him."

They exited the woods near the large granite rock altar that had been the gathering place of the coven several months earlier.

Cat looked down at her phone. "We have five minutes before midnight," she said. "Let's take our places on the circle, so we are ready for the fight."

They climbed up onto the black, granite outcropping and carefully made their way across the steep slope to the bottom. The scar on the rock was still closed, but a wisp of sulfur-steam wound its way up from the scar into the night air.

The Celtic quaternary knot had been carved into the rock face and it glowed with golden light. Cat and Donovan climbed across the scar and took the space on the knot that was due south. Rowan and Henry stood opposite them on the other side of the scar, and Hazel and Joseph stood next to the scar facing east. Wanda stood in the knot facing west. The women lifted their arms to shoulder height and closed their eyes. Electric energy thrummed through the air and the scent of fresh ozone replaced the smell of sulfur. The men, standing just behind their partners, copied their actions and the energy increased. Rushing wind blew around the circle, cleansing the space.

Cat lifted a wand embedded with crystals high above her head, and a trail of light followed her movement. Then she lowered her wand. "I cleanse the space to the south," she called out.

Hazel lifted her own wand, light pouring from the tip, and took a deep breath, summoning the power within her. "I cleanse the space to the east," she cried, lowering her wand.

Rowan lifted her wand, glanced at each of her sisters, then lowered her wand, the stream of light still visible. "I cleanse the space to the north," she said, as the wind increased.

Wanda lifted her wand, glanced around at the sisters, and smiled. "And I cleanse the space to the west," she exclaimed as the wind whipped around her.

Then all of them turned and walked clockwise around the edge of the circle, waving their wands. "We cleanse all places in between," they chanted and then stopped where they started.

Cat cast the first spell.

"We cast this circle, as is our right,

To protect us with thy holy light.

Nothing can harm or corrupt our plea.

As we ask, so mote it be."

Suddenly the ground shook below them. Joseph grabbed hold of Hazel. "Are you okay?" he asked.

She nodded and smiled. "It's just like surfing," she said.

"You know how to surf?" he asked.

She grinned. "No, but I'm sure this must be just like it."

The rock trembled again, this time more like a wave, the earth rolling below their feet. Planting their feet in a wider stance for more balance, they held their wands out like weapons and waited for the next wave.

A low rumble sounded from deep underneath them, vibrating the granite.

"He's coming," Henry called out. "Be strong."

The fissure opened with a hiss of steam and the scent of sulfur warred with ozone.

Donovan, Henry, and Joseph lifted their wands and pointed them toward the opening. Henry cast the second spell.

"We ask for power through this blessed night,

To replace the darkness with the light.

We combine the power of three.

As we ask, so mote it be."

Blue light shot from the wands and merged over the fissure, sparking like a forge against metal. The fissure started to close, the power of the wands scaling the edges.

"We need more magic," Hazel cried out, lifting her wand toward the fissure. She cast the third spell as her sisters and Wanda aimed their wands at the same place.

"To add our partners in this fight,

To overcome darkness with the light.

We add to the power of three.

As we ask, so mote it be."

White light merged with blue and lit the entire circle with power. The crack in the ground seemed to be nearly shut. "It's working," Rowan whispered to Henry, slipping her arm through his. "It's really..."

The ground heaved, and the seven were knocked off their feet onto the hard surface. The fissure split open and a pillar of molten fire shot up into the night sky. Black and orange-red combined to form a demon over twenty feet tall. His head was shaped like a snake, but he had two corkscrew-like horns that were ridged and pointed protruding from each side of his head. His arms were long and sinewy, and his claws were thick and jagged. His eyes glowed with fire and his mouth spewed out lava.

"You thought it would be so easy?" the demon taunted, his deep, thundering voice echoing around them. "You thought casting a circle would contain me? What fools you are."

The rock continued to lurch, like a ship on a rolling sea, and the witches were tossed back and forth, unable to get their footing. Then, a spiderweb of fractures started to form outward from the fissure. The rock cracking and splintering as it moved. Then the granite began to crumble, chunks of rock disappearing into the ever-growing molten lake below them.

"Mom's down there," Rowan screamed.

The rock shook again, and Hazel stumbled forward and fell to her knees. The ground splintered next to her, and Joseph flung himself forward to take the brunt of the scalding steam on his back. He screamed in pain and then the sound changed to a howl as his body reacted instinctively to the injury.

"Joseph," Hazel gasped. "What…"

Yellow irises expanded until the whites were gone and only a small black pupil floated in a sea of amber. His face elongated and his body contorted as man became wolf before her eyes. Then he pulled her into his arms and stood, long claws digging into the rock for purchase. The ground shifted again and the rock beneath them began to crumble.

"Joseph!" Hazel screamed.

With the power of his muscular canine legs, Joseph pushed off the rock and was airborne. Hazel threw her arms around his neck and buried her face in his throat, holding on for dear life. A moment later, they landed on a small outcropping above the pit.

Gasping, she loosened her grip and looked down to where they had just stood. Fiery molten rock had replaced the granite as more of the stone broke away and crumbled into the pit.

"That was close," she gasped.

He gently put her down and changed back to human. "Too close," he said, placing his forehead against hers. "Much too close."

Chapter Sixty-four

The darkness of the cave gave way to the darkness of the night sky. The small group hurried forward, carrying Agnes' unconscious body out of the cave and to a small copse of trees. The ground was soft, and a thick layer of leaves pillowed the earth. "We can stop here," Finias said, his face covered with scratches and soot. "And she'll be safe."

"We're not safe," Dustin said, his shirt torn and a gaping cut across his chest. "And the others are not safe either. Not until the demon's conquered."

"We need to heal her," Seamus said.

Finias shook his head. "No, if we use magic, especially healing magic, it will draw its attention to her," he said. "We can't risk it."

Seamus placed his hand on Finias' shoulder. "It's not our purpose to save Agnes," he said sadly. "But to save the world."

"I don't give a damn about our purpose," Finias whispered harshly. "We need to protect Agnes."

Suddenly a white mist appeared at the edge of the trees and moved toward them. Finias blocked Agnes' body with his own.

"Who are you?" he demanded.

"You had more manners when you were younger, as I recall," a woman's voice replied. "Although, I daresay the situation was far less frightening."

"Mrs. Willoughby?" Finias asked, staring at the ghost before him. "What…"

She turned to Seamus. "Go ahead and heal Agnes," she instructed. "I will block the residual waves of magic."

Seamus knelt down next to Agnes and closed his eyes. He breathed a sigh of relief when he saw that her heart was beating strong, her internal organs were fine, and the injuries she'd taken when the chamber exploded were just superficial, thanks to Dustin's quick thinking of transporting them out of there. He healed the bump on her head, her twisted ankle, and her dislocated shoulder.

When he opened his eyes, he saw her looking up at him and smiling. "Thank you, Seamus," she said. "I feel much better now."

"Well, my dear, I think it's time for you to resume your task."

Agnes whipped around. "Mom?"

Her mother smiled. "Darling, your children need you at the rock face," she said. "I'll meet you up there."

She was turning to Dustin before her mother disappeared. "Dustin, we need…"

"Let's go," Dustin said, and they all disappeared from in front of the cave.

Chapter Sixty-five

The demon turned and stepped from the pit onto the granite, burning welts into the hard stone. It moved slowly toward Cat and Donovan. "And now you, witch," it growled. "You will be the first to die."

Donovan leapt to his feet and raised his wand. "You will not hurt her," he cried, pushing his magic out through the wand. "You will go back to where you came from."

Blue light exploded against the molten pillar; red and blue sparks flew into the air and hissed as they hit the ground.

"Is that all you have?" the demon laughed. "I thought you would have at least tried to make it interesting, Donovan."

Pellets of hot lava shot out of the pillar's hand, like a shotgun blast in Donovan's direction.

"Bacainn!" Hazel cried, sending an invisible barrier between Donovan and the flaming pellets.

The coals hit the wall and exploded, sending sparks in all directions.

"Good job, champ," Donovan called to her.

"Thanks," she replied with an unsteady smile. "There's more where that came from."

While the demon was focused on Donovan, Henry pulled Rowan to her feet and guided her back to the edge of the circle.

"Are you okay?" Henry asked.

Rowan nodded. "Yes, but what can we do? We're outgunned."

Henry nodded. "We just need to keep at him," he said. "Somehow, we'll wear him down."

They both raised their wands, aimed at the glowing figure, and pushed their magic forward. The force knocked the demon to its knees.

"Yes!" Hazel cried as she and Joseph also turned their wands onto the kneeling figure. "He's down now."

Wanda stood and aimed her wand at the demon. "I revoke the protection placed on you by Mistress Wildes," she screamed. "As I wish, so mote it be."

The demon bellowed and turned to face Wanda. He lifted his giant hand and sent it hurtling down towards her. Hazel screamed and pulled Wanda away, having her reappear next to her. "Are you okay?" Hazel gasped.

Wanda threw her arms around Hazel. "Thank you," she breathed. "For a moment…"

The demon turned toward them. "You will not escape me," he said, then he seemed to falter.

"He's weakening," Henry cried out.

Cat stood alongside Donovan and closed her eyes for a moment. "He's not weakening," she whispered to him. "He's baiting a trap."

She sent an urgent thought to her sisters. "Jump back! He's going to attack!!"

Rowan grabbed Henry and Hazel grabbed Joseph and Wanda and pulled them backwards.

"What the hell…" Joseph began, then stopped as large rocks rained down on where they had just been standing.

"Oh, no, you don't," Hazel cried and, with the wave of her hand, sent the boulders sailing into the demon.

The boulders crashed on top of him, and for a moment, there was quiet on the rock.

"Is he? Did we?" Hazel whispered.

Suddenly the boulders were consumed by fire and disintegrated into ash. The demon turned and focused on Hazel. "I killed your mother," it jeered. "And now I will kill you."

Hazel faltered for a moment, then shook her head. "No," she whispered. "No, she's not dead."

"Oh, yes, she's truly dead," he mocked. "And, really, it was your fault. If you'd only been stronger."

"No," Hazel murmured, shaking her head. "No, that's not true."

429

"Your sisters blame you for her death," he continued. "If you'd only done what you were supposed to do, your mother would be alive."

"No," she repeated, her breath hitching in her throat. "No, you're lying."

"They can't bear the sight of you," he persisted. "You killed your own mother."

"No!" Hazel screamed, whipping her wand in front of her and pouring all of her emotion into the power of her magic. Light surged forward, knocking into the pillar with such force that it was knocked to one side.

"My sister did not kill my mother," Rowan screamed and let her emotions flow through her wand, unleashing a second powerful stream.

"You will not divide us," Cat yelled, her wand pouring out light and power that matched the other two.

The pillar was tossed one way and then the other as the streams of light and magic buffeted against it. But it was not diminished.

"We need more," Donovan cried, turning his wand on the demon. "More power."

Henry and Joseph turned their wands on the demon once again, and the pillar turned into a maelstrom of embers, writhing in the center of the circle. The circumference of the pillar grew, and rock melted away, opening up a chasm to a glowing, fiery pit.

"We still need more," Rowan cried, trying to hold her ground at the edge of the circle.

"You have it," Wanda said, sending her power soaring against the demon.

"You cannot defeat me," the demon cried. "For I have legions!"

Suddenly, from the lake of molten lava creatures climbed forth, sliding along the rock face. Their faces held the look of tortured beings, their bodies decrepit and decaying. They crawled over each other, hundreds upon hundreds, as they moved to reach the witches.

Chapter Sixty-six

Suddenly, four more streams of light were added to theirs. Hazel turned around, and tears slid down her face. "Mom, you're okay?" she sobbed.

Agnes smiled at her. "Of course, I am," she said. "Now, pay attention to the legions, dear."

Hazel concentrated on a group of them, then picked them up and dumped them back in the pit.

"Very clever," Dustin said, coming up alongside her. "Do you mind if I give it a go?"

She smiled. "Be my guest," she replied.

Finias stood next to Agnes, fighting alongside her, but he knew that this demonic force was far too powerful for them to defeat. "Agnes," he said. "I don't know how we're going to do this alone."

"But you're not alone," said a voice from behind them.

They turned to see the ghost of Agnes' mother floating above the rock. Finias smiled at her but shook his head. "Even with your help, I can't see…"

"Finias, dear boy, let me finish," she replied. "I brought friends."

Then she stepped over to Agnes and placed her hand on her daughter's shoulder. "I gift you with my energy," she uttered. "Blessed be."

Then, behind her, hundreds of Willoughby spirits lined up, row upon row, and placed their hands on the shoulder of the spirit in front of them.

"Blessed be," was whispered over and over again, a thunderous rumble that shook the circle.

The beam of light from Agnes' wand grew, and energy thundered across the rock against the side of the demon. The maelstrom faltered slightly at this new pressure, but after a few attempts, was able to right itself and continue to spin, destroying more rock and creating a greater hole.

Chapter Sixty-seven

"What are we going to do?" Cat whispered to Donovan. "We don't have anything else."

Suddenly, Cat felt a warm pressure on her shoulder. She glanced back, and her father standing behind her.

"Finias?" she exclaimed. "What?"

"Not just me," he said, motioning behind him with his head. "But generations of Hamiltons fighting with us."

She looked behind him and saw endless lines of spirits, their hands on the shoulders of those in front of them, all focused on her.

"Blessed be," her father whispered with a smile.

"Blessed be," Cat replied, tears of gratitude filling her eyes. Then she felt their combined energy fill her body and merge her spirit with theirs. Focusing, she pushed all of the power into the direction of the wand.

The white light intensified so much that Cat couldn't look directly at it, but the power of her magic stream knocked the pillar to its side.

Then Cat looked over to her sisters and laughed.

"Look behind you," she cried.

Rowan and Hazel turned to see they both had their fathers behind them and generations of their family of spirits backing them up.

Cat turned to Donovan and shook her head in amazement. "That's why we needed three from one," she said. "So, we would have the power of the combined families. So, our ancestors could fight this battle with us."

Blinding light filled the circle, and a wind, ripe with magic, encircled the red glowing embers of the pillar trapping it where it stood.

"Demon of darkness, agent of hell," Cat cried out.

"With the power of love, we vanquish thee," Rowan said.

"In the depths of the netherworld, you shall dwell," Hazel added.

"As we ask," Agnes' voice echoed in the circle. *"So mote it be."*

The pillar collapsed upon itself, swirling inward as it grew smaller and smaller. The legions were swallowed up in the twirling lava as it receded back into the ground. Finally, the demon collapsed, dropping as a cold piece of dark coal into the abyss it had created.

There was complete silence for a moment. Then a soft wind echoed around them, "Blessed Be." And spirits that had lined up behind the circle slowly disappeared, their work complete.

"We need to seal it," Agnes said, walking towards the hole. "To make sure it is trapped forever."

They moved together, circling the chasm, and pointing their wands at the rock. Agnes stepped forward and cast the final spell.

"To seal the creature eternally,
To complete the sisters, legacy,
The way is shut impenetrably,
As I ask, so mote it be."

The granite rumbled, and the crumbled rock pulled together and formed a thick seal over the chasm.

"And now is it time to celebrate?" Seamus asked with a wink.

Chapter Sixty-eight

(Five months later)

"Breathe, breathe, breathe," Joseph coached as Hazel lay on the bed in her room.

"I am breathing," she growled through clenched teeth. "Or else I would be unconscious."

"Which might make this a much more pleasant experience for the rest of us," Cat muttered.

"I'm in labor, not deaf," Hazel called to her sister, who sat across the room.

Rowan chuckled, and Hazel glared at her. "Just wait. In another six months, we all get to see how you're going to handle this."

Hazel closed her eyes as another contraction hit. "Cleansing breath," Joseph coached.

"Too late," Hazel gasped and panted shallowly. "How come they never tell you it hurts in the labor and delivery movies?"

"Because then no one would ever get pregnant," Agnes said, patting the sweat from Hazel's brow. "But you are doing an amazing job."

Agnes looked around the crowded room and sighed. Why in the world Hazel would invite everyone to her baby's birth was beyond her. "Okay, men, except for Joseph. We're getting close to the action time, so all of you to the non-business side of the room."

Finias, Dustin, Seamus, and Donovan moved, so they were up near Hazel's head, offering her more privacy when the actual birth took place. Henry, who had been helping Rowan with healing, stood next to the side of the bed.

"You're doing great," he said, his eyes filled with worry.

"How would you know?" Hazel snarled as she tried to control her breathing. "Have you ever done this before?"

"Well, no, but..." he began.

Finias put a hand on his shoulder and pulled him away from the side of the bed. "You'll be safer back here," he advised.

Hazel exhaled slowly and then took a deep breath. "Are you sure I'm not having a litter?" she asked Joseph.

He leaned over and kissed her on the lips. "It's never happened before," he replied with a grin.

"Actually, from a purely engineering perspective," Dustin said, trying to be helpful. "The probable difficulty is the comparative size difference of maternal and paternal progenitors of the forthcoming infant."

"What?" Hazel asked.

"Joseph's big and you're petite," Donovan explained and shook his head. "That's something you should have discussed before you fell in love."

"And you're bringing that up now because?" she snapped.

Suddenly, Hazel took a deep breath and slowly let it out. "Incoming," she moaned as another contraction took hold.

Joseph took her hand in his and kissed it softly. "You're doing so well," he said.

She gasped for breath and smiled at him. "You want to step in for a moment while I take a break?" she asked.

He met her eyes, but his face was serious. "Hazel, you know I would do anything…"

She inhaled sharply. "Incoming," she gasped, interrupting him. Then her eyes opened wide. "And I want to push."

Rowan hurried to her side and placed her hands on her sister's shoulders. "Okay, sweetheart," she said, smiling down at her. "Now comes the wonderful part. I want you to just relax."

Seamus hurried forward. "Can I help?" he asked, but Rowan shook her head and smiled at him.

441

Instead, Henry walked back to the other side of the bed and gently placed his hand on Hazel's arm.

"I can't relax," Hazel complained. "It hurts…"

She paused for a moment and then smiled. "Hey, this isn't too bad at all," she said. "I can…"

Then she turned and saw the painful grimace on Henry's face. "Henry, no," she insisted.

"Don't worry," Henry groaned. "I can handle it."

"It's only for a moment," Rowan said. "The more you can relax, the faster your contractions will move this little one out of you."

Henry muffled a groan again.

"Are you sure he can handle this?" Hazel asked.

"He said he wanted to do it, in order to understand what I'll be going through with our baby," she said, trying to hide a smile.

"Poor Henry," Hazel said, then her eyes widened, and she nodded. "Outgoing!"

Agnes moved from Hazel's side to the bottom of the bed. "Okay, just the way we practiced," she said.

"Joseph, you move in behind Hazel and support her back. Cat and Rowan hold her legs. Henry, hold on for dear life."

She lifted the sheet to Hazel's knees and examined her. She looked up and met Hazel's eyes. "The baby's head is crowning," she said.

Hazel smiled back, tears flowing freely down her face. Joseph leaned over and kissed her cheek. "You're doing great," he whispered.

"Okay, with this next contraction, bear down and push," Agnes said.

Hazel felt the contraction tighten her abdomen, and she worked with it, concentrating her energies pushing below her navel. "Come on," Agnes urged. "Just a little more. Come on."

Gathering all of her strength, Hazel pushed once more and felt her body push the baby out into Agnes' hands.

A moment later, a tiny cry filled the room.

Agnes looked up, tears filling her eyes, and handed the tiny child to her own baby girl. "Congratulations," she said, her voice hoarse with emotion. "You have a daughter."

Hazel gathered the child to her chest and gazed down at the tiny baby with a head full of dark hair.

Joseph leaned over to stare at his daughter, his eyes gleaming with pride. "Much better than a puppy," he whispered, kissing his wife.

Hazel nodded. "Much better," she murmured, her face glowing with love. She looked up from the baby to the faces of all those she loved in the room. "Family, I'd like you to meet Agnes Willoughby Norwalk. Aggie, I would like you to meet your aunts and your uncles."

Then she turned to her mother, who had tears streaming down her face. "And your grandmother," Hazel said, wiping away her own tears.

"I'm so honored that she's sharing my name," Agnes wept.

"We wouldn't have it any other way," Joseph said. "We wanted to name her after a great lady."

Agnes smiled at Joseph. "Thank you," she said.

Finias came over and hugged Agnes. "Amazing job, grandma," he teased.

She leaned up and kissed him. "This was a miracle," she said. "My life is a miracle."

He nodded. "Our family is a miracle," he said, then a soft thump had him turning away from her and towards the side of the bed. "Not to take away from the moment, but I do need to mention one tiny thing."

"What is it?" Hazel asked, concerned.

"Someone needs to help Henry," he said. "He's passed out behind the bed."

The End

About the author: Terri Reid lives near

Freeport, the home of the Mary O'Reilly Mystery Series,

and loves a good ghost story. An independent author,

Reid uploaded her first book "Loose Ends – A Mary

O'Reilly Paranormal Mystery" in August 2010. By the

end of 2013, "Loose Ends" had sold over 200,000 copies.

She has nineteen other books in the Mary O'Reilly Series,

and books in the following series - "The Blackwood

Files," "The Order of Brigid's Cross," and "The Legend

of the Horsemen." She also has a number of stand-alone

novels and short stories.

Reid has enjoyed Top Rated and Hot New Release

status in the Women Sleuths and Paranormal Romance

category through Amazon US. Her books have been

translated into Spanish, Portuguese and German and are

also now also available in print and audio versions.

Reid has been quoted in several books about the

self-publishing industry, including "Let's Get Digital" by

David Gaughran and "Interviews with Indie Authors: Top

Tips from Successful Self-Published Authors" by Claire

and Tim Ridgway. She was also honored to have some of her works included in A. J. Abbiati's book "The NORTAV Method for Writers – The Secrets to Constructing Prose Like the Pros."

She loves hearing from her readers at author@terrircid.com

Other Books by Terri Reid:

Mary O'Reilly Paranormal Mystery Series:

Loose Ends (Book One)

Good Tidings (Book Two)

Never Forgotten (Book Three)

Final Call (Book Four)

Darkness Exposed (Book Five)

Natural Reaction (Book Six)

Secret Hollows (Book Seven)

Broken Promises (Book Eight)

Twisted Paths (Book Nine)

Veiled Passages (Book Ten)

Bumpy Roads (Book Eleven)

Treasured Legacies (Book Twelve)

Buried Innocence (Book Thirteen)

Stolen Dreams (Book Fourteen)

Haunted Tales (Book Fifteen)

Deadly Circumstances (Book Sixteen)

Frayed Edges (Book Seventeen)

Delayed Departures (Book Eighteen)

Old Acquaintance (Book Nineteen)

Clear Expectations (Book Twenty)

Finders Mansion Mystery Series

Maybelle's Secret

Maybelle's Affair

Mary O'Reilly Short Stories

The Three Wise Guides

Tales Around the Jack O'Lantern 1

Tales Around the Jack O'Lantern 2

Tales Around the Jack O'Lantern 3

Auld Lang Syne

The Order of Brigid's Cross (Sean's Story)

The Wild Hunt (Book 1)

The Faery Portal (Book 2)

The Blackwood Files (Art's Story)

File One: Family Secrets

File Two: Private Wars

PRCD Case Files: The Ghosts Of New Orleans -A Paranormal Research and Containment Division Case File

Eochaidh: Legend of the Horseman (Book One)